Opal]

MW00799375

Her

Broken

Bones

Chapter 1

Jenny braced herself as the police four-wheel drive laboured in thick red mud. The vehicle flicked from road rut to road rut – her head narrowly avoiding a collision with the side window. The Coober Pedy to William Creek Road was soggy, stodgy sludge from days of rain.

A blue pop-up tent, bigrig truck and police vehicle came into view through the mud-covered windscreen. Huddled together on the side of the road, the scene stood out, despite the sheeting rain.

'This is it.' Her new partner, Constable Philips stopped the vehicle at the edge of the road before putting it into low range four-wheel drive. It bucked and jumped as he drove from the rough road to the rugged roadside. Stopping, he turned the motor off and retrieved two oilskin coats from the back seat. Passing one to Jenny, he silently climbed from the driver's seat into knee-deep ooze.

Her initiation into the outback was dry and hot – so hot she thought she might not outlast her new position. Now, after torrential rain, the rich soil was drenched to the point of saturation.

Constable Jenny Williams was used to rain. But where she came from, the grass was green, the hills rolling and the smell of salt breeze never far away. This downpour was like nothing she ever saw before and it was washing evidence away by the second.

Bracing herself, she jumped out, pulled on the coat and slammed the Landcruiser door. Bolting for the makeshift shelter that covered the body of a young woman, Jenny stopped still a moment, struck by the scene.

Wet hair draped across the victim's face. Broken arms and legs stuck out in unnatural positions. Dead eyes stared, almost protruding out of her head, challenging Jenny. She swallowed bile.

'A truck driver saw her body on the side of the road and called it in. That's him over there.' Senior Constable O'Connell pointed to a broad-shouldered, round bellied truck driver who wore work shorts and a blue trucker tank top that failed to cover his midriff.

The rain fell around him, but his eyes were fixed on the body, his face devoid of emotion. Shock settled over him like a blanket. 'You want me to take his statement?' Jenny offered and O'Connell looked from her to Philips before answering.

'No. Philips. You talk to him. See what he knows, then we'll need to bring his truck in to town and check it over. Williams, you can help me gather what evidence we can. We'll need to move this body before forensics can make it on-scene from Adelaide or everything will be washed into the mud.'

'I'll grab some plastic bags from the car. We'll tape them over her hands.' O'Connell's eyebrow rose, but Jenny was moving before he could challenge the idea of bagging the woman's hands.

She worked alongside forensic scientist Penny McGregor before and knew fingernails held all sorts of evidence. Since they couldn't be sure how this woman died, preserving any evidence was her priority.

Returning to the body, a roll of tape ready, she slid the bags on each hand, trying desperately to ignore the bone jutting from the woman's forearm. Despite the heavy rain, blood caked the victim's tank top and cargo shorts.

'Did you get enough photos Sir?' Jenny gazed up at O'Connell who was flicking photos sideways on his mobile phone, zooming in and checking them as he went.

'They'll have to do Williams. I wish it wasn't pissing down. It would make this job a whole lot easier.'

Jenny didn't answer, she returned her focus to gathering evidence. The woman's light coloured hair and fine bones made her think of her missing cousin Melanie. The sole reason she took the job in Coober Pedy was to find out what happened to her cousin and aunt. So far, the trail ended at William Creek Station, the owner dead by supposed suicide.

An ambulance arrived deadly quiet. No sirens blaring, just the strobing red and blue lights casting an eerie glow below the darkened sky. The thunder clouds and driving rain were closing in, emulating the emotions rolling inside Jenny's head. How does a young woman end up dead on the side of a desert road, so far from anywhere?

'I've got a body bag.' Local paramedic Tim ducked under the pop-up tent, the sides running with a river of water that saturated the ambulance officer as he passed beneath.

'Thanks Tim.' Jenny helped him shake off the rain and lay the bag out next to the body as the second paramedic arrived to help.

'We can't use the gurney here.' Tim surveyed the saltbush, shale and deep clay soil. 'I'll need a few extra hands to lift the body into the ambulance.' Tim tried not to shout over the pounding rain as he unzipped the bag. The female paramedic ducked under the foldout tent that swayed and flapped with the wind.

'Emily, this is our new constable. Williams, this is Emily Nowak.'

'Call me Jenny.' Emily smiled as they tried to straighten out the woman's contorted body. Polite conversation and familiar gestures carried on as the dead woman continued to stare. Tim gently pressed her eyes closed.

'I want a perimeter set up around this area.' O'Connell handed a roll of police tape to a State Emergency worker. 'You'll find poles in the boot of the Cruiser over there.' The Senior Constable pointed and the S.E.S. volunteer nodded before trudging through mud to a collect a couple of additional volunteers to aid him.

'We'll need to sieve through this dirt if or when it dries out.' Jenny offered as Tim pulled the zip up around the body that failed to flatten out due to rigor mortis.

'I'll call it in to Adelaide. We'll need to get Penny up here as soon as we can.' Tim secured the victim, ensuring the body bag was watertight.

Jenny's heart leapt at the thought of Penny returning to town. The forensic pathologist was vital in helping solve the murder of Tiffany Cox, but most of all, Penny was one of a handful of people Jenny considered a friend.

It was less than a month since they solved Tiffany's murder. When she first started her new job in Coober Pedy, her boss, Sergeant Mackenzie tried to convince her that the desert town was quiet, with nothing more than the occasional bar fight or claim jump. Tiffany's homicide told a different story. This new death only served to reinforce what Jenny already knew.

This town held the secret to why her cousin and aunt never returned after a holiday in the red centre. But two dead women in one month, that was some sort of record, even for this desolate community.

'I'll ride with the body.' Jenny crouched down by the victim. 'Let me know when Penny is due in, I'll meet her flight.'

'Will do.' O'Connell nodded at her suggestion.

Jenny lifted one side of the body bag, as Tim and Emily grabbed a hold and juggled the awkward, slippery plastic toward the waiting ambulance.

Chapter 2

Jenny shifted from one foot to the other like an excited child waiting for ice cream. Penny's plane taxied down the short runway to the old hardboard and bitumen-clad building that passed for a terminal in outback Coober Pedy. She recalled the day she first arrived, and every day since. The sun pelted down constantly, until this downpour. Not in a million years did she expect it to rain so hard in this arid, scorched desert.

'Penny!' Jenny rushed forward as the forensic scientist entered the terminal. They hugged.

'I'd hoped our next catch up wouldn't be over a body.' Penny glanced past Jenny as she spoke, watching for the tractor and trailer to arrive with her luggage. 'I need to grab my gear.'

'No worries. I'll give you a hand.' Jenny tried not to yell, but the rain on the tin roof made the terminal echo like cheering in a sports stadium. They met the overladen trailer as it pulled up outside. Luggage was piled haphazardly with bags of all shapes and sizes, sheltered under a failing tarpaulin shroud.

'Be careful with that stuff.' She called to the baggage handler. Jenny noted the man was devoid of his usual heavy layer of zinc cream. There was no need. The thunder clouds drowned out the sun entirely and word from the bureau of meteorology predicted it wasn't letting up for another day or so.

They collected two bags each. Jenny led the way out of the terminal.

'You got a spare one of those Driza-Bones for me?' Penny nodded toward the sheet of rain beyond the terminal doors.

'In the car, sorry, should have brought it in with me. I'm not used to this weather. Wait here. I'll go grab it.' Jenny left Penny standing under the awning outside the terminal. Pelting rain ran like a curtain over the tin roof, down a gutterless edge, creating a river running through the dolomite carpark.

Jenny returned a minute later, jumped the torrent of water and held out a second oilskin coat, complete with hood. 'I've never seen it like this out here.' Penny struggled into the stiff material, pulled the hood up and clipped the pop-studs closed on the front before collecting two bags, one in each hand.

'Me neither. Back home on the farm when it rains, it's nothing like this and it's usually bloody freezing.'

'I know. The temperature here is just nuts. It's summer for god's sake.'

'You should see the accident scene. It's like a swamp.'

'I'll process the body and get what I can from the scene, but sounds like there won't be much to find.' Penny forced the rear Landcruiser door open against the wind. Pushing her butt hard against it to hold it in place, she tossed her bags in and waited for Jenny to do the same.

'I did the best I could, but it was pretty hard. Bagged off her hands.'

'Good move.' They rushed to jump in. 'Philips loan you his wheels?'.

'He did. Last I saw him, he was back out on scene with O'Connell trying to figure out what might have happened. One of the S.E.S. guys with a heavy vehicle licence drove the truck into Ted's garage and we'll organise some S.E.S. volunteers to walk the area once this bloody rain stops.'

'What did it look like to you?' Penny flipped the hood back and unbuttoned the front of her coat. They knew there was no point taking it off. Storm clouds surrounded them. The black sky, tinged with iridescent green threatened hail. With a glass of wine, sitting on a covered deck, dry and comfortable, it would have been majestic.

'It was pretty hard to tell. A truck driver spotted the body on the side of the road. She's pretty beaten up, but I'm not sure if that's from a vehicle, or maybe injuries sustained before she died some other way.'

Jenny pulled the Cruiser away from the terminal. Tyres slipped and slid along the red dirt as the road grew boggier from excessive rain and traffic.

'So no one, including the truck driver is admitting to hitting her?'

'Nope, but that road is a common truck route and it links Coober Pedy and the Sturt Highway with the William Creek pub, Nick's station and other properties in the area on the stock route.'

'Oooh. You're becoming a real local with that kind of knowledge.' Penny didn't hide her sarcasm.

'I'm a long way from local still, but I've met a few people.' Jenny bit her lip as she focussed on keeping the vehicle on the slippery road, thankful the police Landcruiser was all-wheel drive.

'Speaking of meeting locals. How's Nick doing?'

Jenny shrugged. She hadn't seen much of Nick. William Creek Station was a long way out of town but they caught up once after Penny left to discuss his father's death and how likely it was that he *didn't* commit suicide.

One of Nick's workmen, Ed identified Melanie from a photo. He was sure he saw her with Nick's dad around the time she disappeared from William Creek pub. Jenny drew a deep breath, recalling how Mrs B. claimed her cousin and aunt left the pub without paying. The nausea in her gut told her they would never willingly abscond.

The only line of enquiry she could follow was Ed's memory, which clashed with everyone else's account and Nick's dad's records, which clearly showed neither her aunt nor cousin ever arrived at the William Creek Station.

Penny stared at Jenny, waiting, but not pushing for an answer. 'I've only seen Nick once.'

'I thought you hit it off.'

'Me too. But I must be reading him wrong. He's given me radio silence since we last talked about his dad's death.'

'Why? Do you think you said something to upset him?'

'Could have. It's a touchy subject. He believes that if his dad didn't kill himself, then his mum, who went missing at the same time, could have killed him.' Jenny flicked the headlights on, the rain reflected in the beam, she dropped them off high beam and squinted as she drove.

'Shit. But that would only make sense if he thought his mum would have reason to kill his dad.'

Jenny licked her lips, her eyes fixed on the road. 'Yeah. I'm not sure why he's jumped to that conclusion. No one has ever mentioned his dad was any threat to his mum.'

'Have you checked police records for domestic violence stuff? Or maybe the hospital?'

'I never seriously considered anything like that. Nick's a cold fish. He's only just gone from stone-cold sulking to even talking to me. I don't want to do anything to make him clam up further. He's my only lead to Melanie and my aunt.'

'Is that the only thing he is?' Penny grinned and Jenny risked taking one hand off the wheel to gently slap her friend's arm.

'Stop it. What's with the matchmaking?'

'It's a lonely place out here Jen. I know I'd be hard pressed to hack it without someone warming up my bed at night.'

'It's usually more than hot enough out here to make do without.' Jenny slowed the vehicle outside the hospital. Stopping, she switched off the engine and pulled the handbrake on. Turning, she studied Penny staring at her, a crease between her eyebrows that said she wasn't buying a word of it.

Chapter 3

The nurse on the front desk glanced up as they entered the hospital, hands full of pathology equipment. It was the same nurse on duty the day she came to interview Sam and Mick about the road accident. The day she literally ran into Nick's rock-hard chest. His steely gaze stared right through her.

'Hey Pat. Busy as usual I see.' Jenny kept her voice light and cheery. The nurse nodded. He was a quiet guy who seemed professional. Jenny only met him a few times over the month, always on duty, never down the pub with Nev and Tim. It made her wonder if he was a loner. Did he have a family?

'Hey Constable.'

'I've told you to call me Jenny.' He shrugged. 'This is Penny, our forensic scientist. She's here to see the body we brought in this morning.'

'Hell of a way to ring in the weekend. She's in the morgue.' Pat went back to his paperwork. Jenny stayed on the spot. He gazed back up, puzzled a moment before he realised she didn't know where the morgue was.

'Oh, sorry. I forgot you're new. It's a pretty small hospital. I use the word morgue loosely. Head out the front, around the side, you'll find a refrigerated shipping container.'

The women stared at each other, mouths open wide. Jenny sighed.

'Best get onto it.' Penny shrugged.

'Thanks Pat.'

The nurse waved without taking his eyes from his paperwork.

The rain eased as they reached the container. A short porch was erected outside the container's rear doors. Penny handed Jenny a pair of disposable overalls and shoe covers.

They removed their shoes and put the covers over their socks, not wanting to dredge mud through the container.

'Let's make this as quick as we can. It's going to be at least minus eighteen in there.' Penny picked up her bag as Jenny opened the door, eliciting a shiver as a blast of freezing air hit her face.

'She was in rigor when we found her.'

'She still is by the looks.' They studied the black body bag a moment. The woman's contorted body caused the outside to sit rigidly, like a canvas swag. 'That gives us a starting point to time of death. Rigor usually passes after eight hours. I'll make sure I pass the info on to Doc Holbrook.'

'How will you transport her to Adelaide?'

'I'll call in an air ambulance with a refrigerated box.'

Penny pulled on a pair of gloves before opening the body bag. Stopping there, she did nothing, simply studied the body and the victim's clothing. She then drew in a slow, steady breath, mumbled something incoherent, then reached in to start work. Jenny marvelled at how the scientist could separate herself so easily. The bright lights of the makeshift morgue clearly revealed the horrible end to the young woman's life.

With her eyes closed, her hair, eyelashes and even the soft hairs on her face white with ice mist, she resembled Snow White, waiting for Prince Charming to kiss her awake. But when Jenny gazed over the woman's body, covered in congealed blood, broken bones pushing through sinew, the reality of death kicked her in the gut.

Averting her eyes, she coughed to clear her throat. 'How old do you think she is?' Her voice was husky to her own ears. She busied herself by getting her phone out to take notes.

'Not even eighteen. Sixteen, seventeen maybe.' Penny's hands stopped for a split second.

'Do you think it's an accident?' Jenny's words were softly spoken. She saw the corners of Penny's eyes crease, her lips rolled and pinched then her hands started working once more.

'Too early to tell. Doc will need to study the injuries. Did you find any ID on her?'

'Nothing. We couldn't find a bag. We collected everything we could from the immediate scene. The S.E.S. crews might find it when we start the search.'

Penny's digital 50mm camera flashed, illuminating the walls of the container along with the victim's face. The click and buzz echoed as the forensic scientist documented every injury from head to toe.

The woman's legs were black and blue with bruising. Penny's camera hovered there a moment, hesitating. 'Did you get photos of the scene?'

'O'Connell did. It was pretty hard with the overcast sky and sheeting rain. It felt like early evening not morning out there with all the thunder clouds around. We didn't have any floodlighting.'

'Looks like she lost her shoes when she was hit.'

'I'll see if the search team can find them.' Jenny added the details to her notes.

'That's weird.' Jenny waited, not wanting to break Penny's concentration. 'Her feet are pretty torn up on the bottom.' She snapped a few shots. 'Doc will have his work cut out for him on this one.'

'Why's that?'

'Some of these injuries are inconsistent with a vehicle impact.' She pointed to the leg bruises. 'And these are a few days old.'

'You believe this is more sinister than a hit and run?' Jenny's fingers were poised over her phone ready to document Penny's answer.'

'I can't say yet. It's freezing in here.' Penny shivered and Jenny did the same, involuntarily. 'Leave me with her for a while and I'll let you know once we are ready to put her on a plane. I want Doc to get to her as soon as possible.'

'Okay.' Jenny was just about to leave when something caught her eye. 'Is that a necklace?'

'Yeah, looks too small for her.' Penny brushed the woman's long hair away from her neck and placed her gloved finger between the chain and the victim's neck. It was a tight fit.

'Is that a crucifix?'

'A tiny one, on a small chain and look at this.' Penny turned over a tiny round gold disc. The engraved name of *Beth* made Jenny take in a quick breath.

Chapter 4

The front door flew open. All heads turned to see Penny stomp into the station, shaking her body under her oil skin, throwing water in all directions like a shaggy dog. Wet long hair sat limp around her face, framing her square jaw. 'She's on her way.'

'Looks like you scored the last of the rain. The experts thought it was going to hang around another day.' Jenny handed Penny a towel.

'It never rains long here. One torrential downpour and the place fills up like a reservoir. Take weeks to drain away.' Philips handed Penny a cup of coffee. From behind him, Jenny screwed up her nose, grabbed her throat with one hand, stuck out her tongue and rolled her eyes. Penny snorted, coughed then reached for the cup.

'Thanks.' She smiled at Philips before taking a sip. Her eyebrows rose just before she shuddered. Jenny supressed a giggle.

'You don't like it?' Philips' lip dropped.

'It's just hot.' She waved her hand. 'All good thanks Philips.' Placing the cup down on the counter, she wrapped the towel around her hair and rubbed. 'Can we get on site yet?'

'Not for a few days at least.' Penny sighed.

'What about the truck?'

'Yep, that's waiting for you at Ted's garage. I'll drop you around there in the morning.'

'I'd rather get on with it now thanks. If that truck hit our victim, I'll find flesh and bone fragments and I'd rather do it before they degrade.' Philips paled. 'What did the truck driver say in his statement?'

'Couldn't get a word out of him. He was shaking and shivering. Puked up twice before I got him to the hospital. Left him there.'

'Do you have his identification?'

'Yep and we have his truck keys.' Philips turned to the desk, pushed a few papers aside then stopped as O'Connell considered him over a new pair of reading glasses, his eyebrow raised. A goofy grin tugged at Philips' lips. O'Connell carefully stacked a pile of papers, picked up a bundle of keys and dropped them into Philips' waiting hand.

'He isn't going anywhere in a hurry.' The constable turned back to Penny, the keys jingled on his finger.

'Do you think he hit her?' Jenny watched Philips take a deep breath, his brows creased.

'Hard to say for sure. To see a girl on the side of a slippery, muddy road in the pouring rain while towing two wild dog trailers behind a bigrig...' He shrugged, his lip lifting with his shoulders. 'That would be bloody miraculous.'

'So, it would have taken all his concentration to stay on the road?'

'That's only my opinion. I've got no solid evidence to back it up.'

'Time to check the truck and see if we can find some then.' Penny abandoned the unfinished coffee, tossed the towel over a chair and made a beeline for the door. 'I'll grab that lift now thanks Philips.'

'I'll join you.' Jenny approached her locker. The door was half open when a gruff voice garnered everyone's attention.

'Williams!' Sergeant Mackenzie scowled from his doorway one hand on the frame, the other on his hip.

'Yes Sir?' She rolled her eyes at Penny who waited by the front door, her hand on the handle, a frown on her face.

'What's this about a necklace?' Sergeant Mackenzie's finger was pointing directly at Jenny, his nostrils flared and the vein in his forehead pulsed. 'You've issued a bulletin without my approval.'

Jenny's eyes pleaded with O'Connell. 'I gave her the go-ahead Sarge.' The sergeant stepped forward, crossed his arms and puffed out his chest. O'Connell continued. 'Is that a problem?'

'Just give me a report.'

'The necklace is small Sir, like a child's.' Jenny's heart was racing. Why did she have to explain herself all the time? 'It was likely a gift she wore all the time. It's *our* assumption someone probably listed it in last known clothing and effects of a Missing Person's Report.'

'So I issued a *BOLO* on it.' O'Connell jumped to her rescue.

'Did you run Missing Persons for the first name before stuffing around with that?'

Sergeant Mackenzie was on her case the moment she arrived. He accused her of showboating, trying to make a name for herself to further her career. When she pushed him to escalate the last case, he shut her down.

Even after uncovering the former Senior Constable was involved and saving her boss from a bullet to the brain, he wouldn't cut her any slack.

Jenny bit her lip. 'We did sir. There was a long list of missing women with the name Elizabeth or Beth of all ages and we are going to go through them one by one to see if we can find the necklace mentioned, or a description that matches our victim, but I thought that anyone who was working a Missing Person's case that involved this necklace would remember it instantly.'

Her adrenalin was firing now. Her hands flew to her hips. 'Especially if we highlighted it.'

Sarge pursed his lips, fidgeted and opened his mouth to speak. O'Connell intervened.

'Did you find anything helpful under the bagged hands Penny?'

'That was bloody quick thinking on William's part Sir. I pulled out lots of samples. Mostly dirt, but if there's any trace evidence, we'll find it. I'll know more once the lab gets it. I've sent the samples with the body.'

Sergeant Mackenzie gaped at Penny, then O'Connell before his eyes rested on Jenny's. He huffed, turned and moved back to his office, slamming the door.

Penny's mouth was open. She scanned the faces, and strode toward O'Connell's desk. 'What's his problem? Why is he so hard on Jenny?'

'I'm not sure, but I think it has something to do with his daughter.' They all glanced at the Sergeant's door. Philips shuffled from one foot to the other, jostling by the door still.

'He told me once I reminded him of her.' Jenny collected her vest and checked her weapon out.

'I'm not surprised. You don't look anything like her Williams but by god, your attitude could be a reincarnation of Lily's. That girl had spunk, but her death nearly killed him too.'

'You two ready for a lift now?' Philips shoved his hands in his pockets and stared out the glass doors as he waited.

Jenny pushed thoughts of the Sergeant and his daughter aside. They needed to focus on their victim. Why was a young woman out in the desert with no shoes, no handbag and no food or water?

'Did we find any abandoned vehicles in the area?' she asked Philips as they left the station.

'Not yet. We'll get back out there and search as soon as we can.'

'I'll join you. This case is weird and I'm sure we are missing something. I'm just hoping what we need didn't get washed away with all the rain.'

Chapter 5

Philips waved from the Landcruiser as he pulled away from Ted's garage. There was no escaping the mud as they trudged through the carpark and into the open bay of the garage. A bigrig with metallic green paint and silver pinstriping was parked up out of the rain.

The dog trailers were parked outside, covered in mud, the smell of cattle hung in the air. Empty now, Jenny was thankful they weren't cluttered with livestock when the driver found the victim.

'Where do we start?' Jenny held up the scientist's tool chest.

'Put that down at the front of the truck. If our victim hit this truck, then we'll find evidence in the grill.'

'Sounds horrible.'

'It is what it is.' Penny squatted in front of the vehicle and retrieved a black light from a leather bag. 'Can we kill the lights? This will be the easiest way to start looking for tissue.'

Jenny suppressed a shudder. Realisation that pieces of their victim could be hanging from the grill made her blood curdle. She scanned the area, found the light switches and crossed the garage to the far wall. Gingerly she reached for the panel of switches. Using one finger, she attempted to avoid the grease stains as she flicked the switch marked 'Main Garage.'

The lights clicked out. She pulled her flashlight from her vest, switched it on and made her way back to Penny. The forensic scientist waved a purple light in her gloved hand. As it passed over the front of the truck, a fluorescent glow set an eerie scene.

The vehicle loomed over Penny's near six-foot frame like a monstrous clown mask. The headlights stared out, and the grill reflected light, emulating a toothy mouth like the gates of Luna Park in Melbourne.

'Bingo.' Penny reached for her camera. Holding it up in the light beam within Jenny's reach. 'Can you take a couple of pics for me?'

'Sure.' Jenny stepped closer, with no desire to see fragments of human flesh, yet realising this was part of the job.

She shoved the flashlight into her back pocket. It shone through her trousers casting a glow behind her. Reaching for the camera, she turned to focus on where Penny held the light.

The camera automatically shot a series of photos with the push of a button. Flashes of sudden light strobed over the clown face, joining the purple iridescent glow of the black light to create a spooky vibe. Jenny clenched her jaw and ignored the tingle running up her spine.

'Will anything have survived the rain?'

'On the outside, unlikely, but anything embedded deep enough into the truck grill or around the lights should be usable. The truck would have been doing between sixty to eighty kilometres , even in the rain. The force of impact on our petite victim's frame would have sent blood, bone and body tissue deep into the vehicle's crevices.

'I don't envy you this job.' Jenny stopped taking photos. 'Is that enough?'

'Yep, hit the lights and we'll see if we can retrieve some samples.' Jenny pulled her torch from her back pocket and returned to the bank of light switches. One click and the room flooded with bright fluorescent lighting once more. Illumination did nothing to ease the queasiness in her stomach.

She watched as Penny used long, pointed stainless steel tweezers to pick up what appeared to be a bone fragment from around the passenger's side light. She placed it into a small envelope, sealed the top and marked it with the case number and date.

Another search revealed an elongated piece of sinew. Spots of blood dotted the surface. Jenny held her stomach and swallowed the bile in her mouth as Penny removed the human remains with painstakingly slow and precise movements. Penny's brow creased as she lowered it meticulously into another evidence bag and sealed it.

'Is that what I think it is?'

'Yep. Looks like you'll need to interview the truck driver again. This time, you should push him for answers. I'll send the samples away for DNA sampling, but that takes a while. We'll get a blood type match relatively quickly which should be enough to push the guy for answers.'

'Damn. I was hoping he was just being a good Samaritan.'

'At least he called it in. He could have just kept driving.'

'What was she doing out in the middle of nowhere?'

Penny shrugged. 'Not my department. I find the evidence, you find out the who and why.'

Chapter 6

Jenny leant against the shower wall, wishing the hot water could wash away more than the mud and sweat of a long day.

The cold, lifeless body in the morgue was tolerable. It wasn't her first time in a pathology suite. Her upbringing grounded her too. Dead calves ravaged by foxes, their eyes torn from the sockets and maggots crawling from flesh was part of daily life. She considered herself tough, seasoned by the farming life – growing up understanding life and death, but this was different. Watching Penny carefully pick pieces of the girl's flesh from the truck grill evoked emotions she never felt before.

She scrubbed her hair, her body and tried to scrub her mind clean, but the broken, contorted body of the young woman kept appearing whenever she closed her eyes.

Shaking herself free of the images, she turned off the shower and stepped out, thankful that steam covered the mirror, because looking in it right now would only amplify her guilt.

The young woman's features made her think of Melanie. Memories of her cousin were always mixed with loss and guilt. Why Melanie? How does a young woman just about to embark on her university years go missing without a trace?

She combed her wet hair and tied it back in a ponytail, not bothering to blow dry it. Her personal belongings arrived early in her second week, but her trusty blow dryer was yet to see the light of day. It seemed too indulgent to spend any time on herself when she should be dedicating every spare moment to tracking what happened to her cousin and aunt.

Dressed, she left her room to meet Penny and her new friends in the Motel bar. She should have been happy, but instead, melancholy set in. Melanie never got a chance to finish her school years and grow up. Or was she wrong? Melanie and Aunt Carolyn were officially missing, but that didn't mean they were dead. Did it?

Noise hit her, forcing her mind back to the present as she pushed open the door to the bar. Doctor Nev and Paramedic Tim sat along the bar next to Penny, looking relaxed and comfortable like one of the guys. There was no hint of the horrors the forensic scientist endured today.

Jenny envied Penny's casual, happy-go-lucky attitude. She fought with her own need to control most situations. Not exactly sure why or when she developed the habit. Maybe losing Melanie when they were in high school sparked the beginning of her need to keep everything in her life measured and on a tight leash.

Would solving Melanie and her Aunt Carolyn's case change that? She didn't think so. It was too late now anyway.

Penny waved when she spotted her, a spare beer already in her hand. She watched Nev lift a jug of beer from the bar as all three turned and wandered through the tables towards her.

'Let's grab a table, I'm starving.' Penny pointed to a long table in the middle of the room where her new partner Philips and his wife Dianna sat with their son Tommy.

The boy seemed to be growing like a weed, his straight blonde hair cut in a home styled bowl bob swayed like a wave; when he turned quickly to look at them, a wide grin crossing his face.

'Dianna. How are you?' Jenny made sure she made eye contact with Philips' wife. Her lip reading was excellent, but Jenny's signing was atrocious so understanding the reply wasn't easy.

'Hi yourself Constable.' Jenny's eyes drifted to Danny as he translated for his wife. Philips, or Danny when they were off duty, was a doting husband and dad and she felt a little guilty about giving him such a hard time when they first met.

She misunderstood his protective nature as him being condescending because she was a woman. Penny pointed out he was just that kind of guy. The experience taught her a valuable lesson. She now tried hard not to mistake chivalry for chauvinism.

Watching him with his wife now, brought a smile to her face. He genuinely was just a nice guy.

'How's Tommy's kindy going?' Jenny sat down across from Dianna as Penny handed over a schooner of beer.

Dianna signed so quickly. There was no hope of her understanding. She knew she was frowning, but it must have been serious looking because Dianna stopped to study her.

'He's enjoying it but not as much...' Danny stopped speaking, and shifted gears. 'Why?' He was looking at his wife, confusion on his face. He nodded as Dianna signed another sentence and turned to Jenny. 'Dianna asked if you're okay? You look stressed.'

Jenny laughed. 'I was just concentrating. I've been trying to learn how to sign.' She watched Dianna as she spoke.

Dianna laughed, the sound strange coming from the lips of a woman who never spoke a word. 'I'll teach you.' Danny spoke and Jenny wasn't sure if that was Dianna offering or Danny, but either way, the answer would be the same.

'That would be great.'

Dianna signed and Danny picked up where they left off. 'I'm enjoying the downtime more than Tommy is enjoying kindy.'

'I bet you are.' Jenny sipped her beer and turned to Penny. 'You said you found something helpful?'

'I did. That necklace, the nametag part. There was a date on it. It was well worn so I missed it at first, but I'm assuming it was her first communion date. It fits with the victim's estimated age.'

'What was the date?'

'That's the weird bit. It's dated in US format, you know month, day, year.'

'You think she's American?'

'I think we might need to widen our search of missing persons.'

'Is this about that hit and run from this morning?' Nev leant in to overhear the conversation.

'Yeah. We've not identified her yet.'

'That sucks.' He drained his beer, then stared into the glass as he put it down.

'Big time. Someone out there has lost their daughter and we can't even tell them we've found her.'

'The truck driver was pretty messed up. We sedated him.' Jenny didn't share why the driver would have been so shaken. Penny exchanged a quick glance which Nev must have picked up. He went to say something but Danny interrupted.

'You know we've not seen a suspicious death here for years Williams. Then you rock up and there's been two in a month.'

'It's nothing to do with me. Like I told you with Tiffany's case, there were zero homicide cases at my old station in Victor. Besides, Tiffany's death was six months before I arrived.'

'I've managed to take a few days of leave while we wait for the scene to dry out, saves flying home and back again next week.'

Jenny was thankful Penny changed the subject because wondering if Danny seriously considered her a murder magnet wasn't pleasant. She already bore the responsibility for not finding Melanie and Aunt Carolyn. The last thing she needed was to believe a death curse followed her around.

Thinking of curses reminded her she needed to catch up with Nev's Uncle. It seemed he believed a dark cloud hung over William Creek Station. She wasn't sure it was relative to her enquiries, but she wanted to find out in any case.

'I figured I could help you house hunt while I'm here?' Penny's voice snapped her out of her daydream.

'Somewhere close to good coffee.' Jenny involuntarily glanced Danny's way as she mentioned coffee.

'What are you saying about my coffee?' He looked wounded.

'Nothing Danny. I'm just a coffee snob and rather than drink instant at the station, I'd rather stop off in the morning on the way to work at a coffee shop. So, I need a place close to work and good coffee.'

Jenny spent over a week finding the time to make her way to the main street of Coober Pedy. Up until then, every waking hour was consumed with working, tracking down her cousin's movements or eating and drinking in the Motel pub.

'There isn't a lot to rent in town.' Nev drained his beer and reached for the jug. 'There's a spare room at our place.' His gaze settled on Tim who nodded agreement.

'You guys share a place?'

'Yeah. We've got a dugout on the outskirts of town.' Nev topped up Jenny's beer without asking.

'But I don't have wheels so I need to be in walking distance to the station.'

'We can carpool. Between us we have a car each and Tim and I share the same shift most of the time. You can use my car when we are on nights. Or I've got a mountain bike you can borrow.'

'I don't know guys. I appreciate the offer but I was kind of hoping for something in town.'

'You won't find dugouts to rent in town. All of the mines in town have been converted to accommodation or commercial places.'

'Damn.'

'We can look around and double check, just in case. It will be fun.' Penny grinned, her eyes twinkled mischievously. Jenny's mood picked up a notch.

'I'm sure you're right Nev, but we'll check out the rentals in town and then I'll let you know after the weekend. If that's okay?'

'Sure.'

'Besides, a girl has to have an excuse to go shopping. Right?' Jenny checked with Penny, a matching grin from ear to ear lifted her spirits. It was going to be a good weekend. Not that there was much in the way of clothing stores in Coober Pedy – unless you counted cowboy boots and flannelette shirts.

'I'll stay until Monday and if it isn't dry by then, I'll fly back and return when it is.'

'Fingers crossed the renowned Coober Pedy sun comes back out in full force.'

'Be careful what you wish for.' Nev raised his beer in salute as everyone laughed.

'Oh, almost forgot. Can you organise that catch up with your uncle?'

Nev nodded over his glass. 'I'll find out if he's around.'

'Great. Just let me know when.'

'Will do. I'll grab another jug.' He pushed his chair back.

Chapter 7

'State your name for the recording.' Jenny sat alongside Philips in the cramped interview room. The truck driver's bulk filled an entire side of the desk. His tattooed shoulders and arms leant on the table, his head hanging down as he sucked in a slow, steadying breath.

'Brett Hagan.'

She confirmed he was the driver of the vehicle impounded earlier, then pushed on with the interview.

'Tell us what happened yesterday morning Mr Hagan, Friday the sixth February two thousand and fifteen.' Jenny watched Philips take written notes as she conducted the interview.

Brett's top lip quivered. He sniffed, then rubbed his nose with the back of his hand. His eyes glistened with unshed tears, but Jenny wasn't backing down. Despite any remorse the driver might be experiencing, she needed to do her job.

'I don't know.' Jenny waited for him to compose himself, but when he didn't continue she pushed on.

'You called triple zero Mr Hagan.'

'I did?' Brett's eyebrows rose, his eyes scanned from her to Philips and back again.

She frowned, considering if he genuinely couldn't recall the accident. Shock could do strange things to people's memory but she needed to push on.

'Do you recall hitting her Mr Hagan?'

'No.' The colour drained from his face.

'We found human tissue in the front grill of your truck Mr Hagan. You need to tell us what happened, or you'll be facing charges of manslaughter.'

He stared at her, his chest heaving like he might throw up any moment. Finally, the dam broke. Sobbing like a child, his whole body shook. Jenny squirmed, uncomfortable with the sudden show of emotion.

Philips calmly spoke through the man's tears. 'It's okay mate. We just need to know what happened. It's obvious you didn't deliberately hit her.'

Brett struggled for composure as Jenny reached for a box of tissues and passed them over the table.

'We know it's all a lot to take in Mr Hagan, but It's important that we piece together how this young woman ended up being hit by your truck.'

'She just came out of nowhere.' He stopped talking to blow his nose, the sound comical amongst the tension in the room. 'It took me a hundred metres to pull up.' Another blow. 'Why the hell did she jump out like that?'

Jenny regarded Philips whose face mirrored her thoughts. *Suicide by truck, not a nice way to go.*

'Are you saying she deliberately threw herself in front of you?'

'I don't know. Like I said, she came from nowhere. It was raining. Visibility was bloody shocking. By the time I caught sight of her, it was too late to do anything. I swerved, but that sound, I'll never forget that sound.' He tore the tissue to pieces in his hand.

'You did the right thing calling the police Brett.' Philips rounded the table and patted the driver on the shoulder, his hand dwarfed by the man's bulk. 'The crash unit will assess the site today, now that the rain has finally stopped and we have forensics working on the victim. Is there anything else you remember that might help us identify the girl?'

'I don't think there's anything else I can tell you.' His eyes searched the room as though they were trying to claw information from the bare grey walls.

Finally, he shook his head slowly, pulled anther tissue from the box and sighed. The sight of the big, burly driver shaking with silent tears spoke to Jenny's soul. She believed he didn't hit the girl intentionally, but she needed to keep an open mind and he was going to have to stay in town for now.

A sinister thought pushed into her mind. She studied the man carefully, considering if the question was warranted.

'Have you ever seen the young woman before Mr Hagan?' He shook his head. 'You'll need to speak for the recording.'

'No. Never.'

'So she wasn't hitch hiking in your truck? She didn't flee any unwanted advances?'

His entire body went rigid. His mouth opened and closed, before words finally spilled out. 'No bloody way. Even if I picked her up, I'd never touch her like that.'

'We've yet to search the inside of your truck. Will we find her shoes, her handbag maybe?' She watched him closely for any sign of fear or anxiety. Instead, he lifted his chest high, proudly, drew a steady breath and stared her straight in the eyes.

'I have a fifteen-year-old daughter.' He continued to hold her gaze.

'Stay close Mr Hagan. We need to continue with our enquiries and we are still awaiting your drug tests. We'll need to see you again before we can release you and your truck.' She braced for an argument over time off the road and lost income, but the driver simply shrugged as if that was the least of his worries.

'Interview ceased at nine-forty-five.' She pressed *Stop* on the recording and got up to escort the driver from the interview room.

'I'll log him out.' Philips' face was set in a scowl.
Jenny opened the door and held it for the driver. She knew
Philips didn't appreciate her line of questioning.

'Thanks Philips.' She tried to make eye contact, but his
gaze was fixed on the driver who looked like he was the one hit
by a truck.

'I've got some paperwork to catch up on.' She added
lamely as she followed him out and into the main office. The
thought of the paperwork she needed to do tore her mind away
from any guilt over the driver or Philips' sensibilities. She
planned also, to pull Nick's family history, including what she
could find out about his dad's suicide.

'Where's Penny?' O'Connell asked as she returned to
the front office. She watched Philips lead Brett Hagan over to
finish writing up and signing his statement. Her partner patted
the big man on the back as they huddled at the front counter.

Jenny approached O'Connell's desk, not wanting to
discuss the case within earshot of the driver.

'She's doing a final check on the truck and then we'll
catch up for lunch. Can we get out to the scene yet?'

'No. The road is still almost impassable. The crash
investigation unit finished up this morning and they said it was
hard going on the way back into town. The road is shot to
pieces.'

'So we've got Sunday off?

'At this stage, yes, but if it dries out earlier than
expected, we'll head straight out. Otherwise, Monday morning,
first thing. I've notified the S.E.S and C.F.S. volunteers to help
us out. The Country Fire Service offered extra help to make
sure we find out where the girl came from. The crash scene is
miles from any homestead.'

'Okay. Any hits on an ID yet?'

'Nothing. I've widened the search, as you suggested, but international cases take time and way too much red tape to get any quick answers.' Jenny nodded before turning to get back to the files she needed. 'How's your other investigation going?'

O'Connell was the only person other than Nick and Penny who knew why Jenny was drawn to Coober Pedy to begin with. So far, her secret was safe, but now she was digging into Nick's case she wondered if she should keep him informed.

'Nothing more yet. I spoke with the rest of Nick Johnston's workers, even the ones who have moved on, but only Ed could confirm my cousin was ever there.' Jenny leant in close again.

'What next?'

'It's a long shot, but Nev's uncle claims William Creek Station is cursed so I'm considering interviewing him. Maybe there's a link to what happened to Melanie. She was seen out at the station by Ed, but no one else.'

'Good luck Williams, but don't let this investigation distract you. Sarge will drag us both over the coals otherwise.'

'Got it Sir. I'll be discrete.' Jenny stepped away as Philips escorted the truck driver out the front door, returning a moment later.

'That has to suck big time.'

'What?'

'Having that girl run out in front of you like that and not being able to do anything about it. A truck with two dog trailers takes ages to stop and with that mud.' Philips shook his head sympathetically.

'If that's what happened. Let's make sure Penny doesn't find anything the girl owned in his truck before we assume it was just an accident.'

O'Connell glanced up from his desk. 'That and the autopsy report. We need all the information before we can let the guy leave town.'

Philips sighed. His great big heart was easily swayed by a few tears. Discovering his former Senior Constable covered up Tiffany's murder was hard on him.

She resisted the urge to feel sorry for him. Danny seemed to enjoy the simple life, living in the bush. His wife was lovely and Tommy was a cute kid. What more could the guy wish for? Jenny envied him. She knew she would never know that level of contentment. At least not until she found her cousin and aunt.

Chapter 8

Jenny almost shivered as the smell of freshly brewed coffee hit her senses. So far, Coober Pedy produced a lot of surprises, but none was more welcome than finding Nikolic's café in the main street.

'Hi Niko. I've brought a friend. This is Penny.' A dark-haired man, in his early thirties waved from behind the counter.

'Constable Williams. Good to see you.' His Serbian accent was charming, that along with his deep brown eyes and olive complexion, gave away his European heritage the moment anyone met him.

'Call me Jenny Niko.'

'Of course.' The dimple on his cheek told her he wasn't about to call her by her first name anytime soon. 'Lovely to meet you Miss Penny.'

'Can I have my usual thanks Niko. Penny what will you have?'

'Same as you. I'm not fussy.'

'I drink a double latté with a generous helping of caramel syrup. You might want to rethink that.'

'That's disgusting.' Penny screwed up her nose. 'How can you destroy good quality coffee like that?'

Niko nodded in agreement but that didn't make Jenny uncomfortable over her sugary latté. She knew it wasn't everyone's favourite, but she loved the mix of sweet and bitter.

'That's why I warned you.'

'Fair call. I'll have a double espresso thanks, short as you can make it.'

'Ah, the lady knows how to truly drink her coffee.' Niko left the table, returning to the counter to start their order.

Jenny led Penny to a table by the door. Alfresco dining was pointless in Coober Pedy's main street. The streets were wide, lined with ample parking for caravans and trucks but even with a layer of bitumen, red dirt drifted in with every passing car.

Niko's café featured a handful of tables and chairs out front, only used as a spot to wait on takeaway orders or by a handful of weathered locals who loved to watch the tourists come and go.

Today, patchy clouds allowed the sun to pelt down on the still wet soil. The humidity was skyrocketing. Jenny hovered by the window air-conditioner and waited a moment for the sweat to evaporate from her face.

'It's going to be a muggy few days until this moisture disappears.'

'Then you'll be whingeing it's dry and hot again.' Penny teased as she sat down at the small square wooden table. Jenny wondered if the distressed white paint was made that way to suit the décor of the rough, weatherboard shack or if it was genuinely a recycled piece.

'So what's Niko's story?' Penny asked as Jenny dragged herself away from the chilled air to take her seat.

'His dad is the Priest at the local Serbian church, just up the road.'

'He's pretty cute for a preacher's son. Is he attached?'

'Ask him yourself.' Jenny nodded as Niko came closer, two coffees balanced carefully.

For a split-second Jenny thought her friend would indeed ask, but thankfully, she let her curiosity die with the smell of strong coffee.

'Thanks Niko.' Jenny smiled.

'Are you ladies eating?' He put two menus down on the table.

'Sure. Give us a minute to decide.' Jenny watched Niko nod and leave. 'You shock me Officer McGregor. I thought you'd ask him for sure.'

'Tempting, but this case has me a little stumped and my mind wouldn't be clear enough to make the most of that body.' She cooed, making Jenny giggle.

'I thought none of this ever got to you.' Jenny sipped her coffee, closing her eyes a second to savour the taste.

'Usually no. But this one gives me the heebie-jeebies. She's so young and why was she alone, barefoot in the middle of the outback?' Penny scanned the menu without seeing it.

'Did you find anything in the guy's truck?'

'Nothing belonging to a woman. I can still taste the smell of the long dead socks I found in his sleeping cab, but there wasn't even a tiny sign of a female passenger. No bag, no shoes, no perfume, nothing. There were a few prints that didn't match his, but they weren't small enough to belong to the victim.'

'But you've sent them to the lab to run?' Jenny spoke quietly as Niko scooted past toward the veranda, a takeaway order in his hands. She watched him hand it to a grizzly looking miner as a truck roared down the main street, making Penny wait to answer her question.

'Of course, but I doubt anything will come of them. The truck, other than the outside where the girl was struck, was clean of any sign of her.'

'So she ran across the desert and what, jumped out in front of the truck to kill herself?'

'Or she was so desperate to find help and didn't realise the truck couldn't stop fast enough?'

The two women sat quietly a moment, staring at the menus and sipping their coffee, both lost in their own thoughts.

'Enough death.' Jenny finally broke the silence. 'I'm starving and we have some house-hunting to do.'

'Are you seriously considering moving in with Nev and Tim? That could prove a little tempting. I know it would for me.' Penny smiled.

'Only if I can't find my own place. Besides, Nev and I are just friends. He's okay with that.'

'And you're sure about that?'

Chapter 9

The vibe in the front bar of the Motel matched the sodden, wet soil outside. The huge space, part restaurant, part bar was eerily empty with a handful of straggly, wet, bored patrons lining the dark wood timber bar, all talking in hushed tones.

'Nearly all the local roads are still closed. Painted Desert Road is a river of mud.' Tim offered his local expertise, beer in hand, smile wide. His strawberry blonde hair and freckled face made Jenny think of her dad, whom she needed to call. She pushed the thought aside.

'I heard nearly twenty poor sods are stranded out by the Pink Pub on the Oodnadatta Track.' Nev picked up the empty jug and shook it in the air. 'Anyone for a top up?'

'I don't know Nev. It's been a long day. I'm ready to hit the sack.' Jenny wasn't only physically exhausted, she was emotionally spent. Four hours, six houses and not one liveable place amongst them.

'Beer will cheer you up,' he offered, and Penny patted her on the back as Nev strode off toward the bar.

'At least you have options.' Her city friend smiled knowingly and Jenny's mind wandered to Nev's butt in his tight denim jeans. She shook her head and Penny laughed.

'Maybe I should just stay at the Motel?'

'Didn't find anything nice then.' Tim's grin said he already knew the answer to his questions.

'The first place was a tin shed. Hot as hell even after all this rain. On a regular hot summer day, it would be like living in a furnace.'

'How about that *dugout*.' Penny used air quotes over the word.

'Well I've seen a few of the local dugouts and technically they *did* qualify. A mound of dirt with a hole dug into it, but this one was even worse than Mark or Mrs Carson's hovel.'

Jenny held out hopes of seeing an attractive dugout worthy of a postcard rather than a working mine with a shack like living space complete with worn gates in lieu of a front door and nineteen-fifties sinks and stoves.

'Bit of a house snob then?' Nev overheard Jenny's last sentence as he placed the full jug of beer in the middle of the table, condensation already dripping down the outside.

Jenny noticed Cheryl over his shoulder. She wiped the front bar and forced a smile when one of the locals placed an order. Slowly, the life was coming back to the barmaid after Tiffany's murder had been solved, but she still missed her best friend. Jenny caught her eye, and waved at the full busted waitress, who smiled weakly.

She drew her eyes back to Nev as he refilled her glass. 'I always thought I was pretty down to earth. The farmhouse I lived in as a kid wasn't anything to get excited about but there were no rats, roaches or deadly spiders lurking to eat me at night. These places were feral Nev.' She screwed up her nose for added effect.

'Our place is still available.' Jenny read between the lines. Nev was promising to be on his most best buddy behaviour but was it Nev she didn't trust? There was no doubt a spark flew between them when they first met, but she snuffed it out quick smart.

Then there was the fact that she fancied getting closer to Nick Johnston, but no matter how they might share a mistrust of the handling of their family police investigations, there was no breaking down the aloof guy's barriers.

Did she want to spend the next however many years it took to find Melanie and Aunt Carolyn, all on her own?

'Okay. I really appreciate the offer. I'm just not sure living on the outskirts of town is my thing, but given the circumstances, I'm willing to give it a go if you guys are.'

Tim and Nev exchanged looks that said they were and Nev raised his beer into the air. 'To new housemates and great times.'

The glasses tapped together and Jenny drew a mouthful of beer, her mind drifting to indigenous paintings in the caves of the escarpment on William Creek Station. A chill ran down her back.

It didn't matter if Nick welcomed her back to his remote property or not. She was going to force herself to ignore his crystal blue eyes and focus on finding out more about her family mystery. She needed to get back out to there, soon.

There was just one problem. The road was impassable for at least another few days and the frustration of not being able to do anything made her chest tighten. Or was that just the effect Nick Johnston was having on her?

Chapter 10

Jenny felt like the weekend whizzed by way too fast, but she was grateful she and Penny enjoyed some great times moving what little gear she owned into Nev and Tim's place. The dugout was quaintly decorated with restored colonial furniture and light coloured furnishings. It renewed her hopes of finding a picture-perfect dugout in what was supposed to be a town full of them.

Jenny sipped her coffee from Niko's café. The aroma and taste making her smile inside and out. Niko's little piece of Serbian heaven was her morning treat, one that got her out of bed on a hot and humid day in the desert.

'How did the move go?' Philips wandered from the lunchroom, nodding a greeting to O'Connell as he passed by.

'Good. We are still getting our routine organised. Nev and Tim are on an early day shift this week, so they dropped me off at Niko's and I walked here.' She held her cup aloft.

'Is my coffee really that bad?'

'It's not you Philips, it's me.' She grinned at how the saying went and Philips chuckled. 'No in all seriousness. There is nothing good anyone can do to instant coffee to make it drinkable to a real bean loving girl. Once you start, you can never go back.'

'Good thing I haven't started then.' Philips lifted his instant coffee in a reply salute then took a long savouring sip. Jenny resisted the urge to cringe.

'Doc is starting on our victim this morning.' Penny sat on the corner of O'Connell's desk. 'Can we get on site yet?'

'There is limited access.' Sergeant Mackenzie's deep voice interrupted the casual conversation as he strode into the main office.

'Good. I don't want a swarm of volunteers out there until I've gone over the scene anyway.' Penny sculled her coffee and threw the disposable cup in the bin next to O'Connell's desk.

'I've organised a tracker to meet you out there.'

'Thanks Sarge.' Penny saluted. 'The victim must have come from somewhere close by. The lab is running her clothing for traces evidence. I don't think they'll find much, but we can live in hope. What I did notice is that the fibres were thin. The lab has estimated she's been wearing the same clothing for a while.'

'How long is a while?' Jenny interrupted. 'All I could see when we put her in the body bag was blood and dirt.'

'I don't know, but the fabric was well worn.'

'That could just mean she was poor.' Philips added.

'Whoever she is, she's been missing since she was very young.' All eyes fell on O'Connell who was tapping keys at his computer.

'Report.' Sarge crossed his arms over his chest and waited while O'Connell continued to read.

'We finally have a hit on our Missing Person Report. Our girl is Elizabeth, known as Beth Thompson. Born in Orange County USA in nineteen-ninety-nine. She was reported missing from an outback tour in August two thousand and ten.'

Jenny's blood ran cold as she thought about Melanie and her aunt's disappearance. Four years after they went missing. Could the cases be connected? On one hand, she hoped they were. 'How old was she then?' Jenny did a quick calculation. 'Eleven, twelve maybe?'

'The report says eleven.' O'Connell tapped a few more keys. 'I've got her parents' details here. Do we notify them?'

He studied his commanding officer. The sergeant rubbed his chin, his chest rising with a deep breath. This case was close to home for him. Losing his daughter in a car accident nearly broke him.

He bit his lip, forcing the pain down into a safe place, away from prying eyes. 'Not yet. We should confirm with DNA first. The girl could have stolen the necklace or found it. Did anyone have a sample on record?'

A few more keys tapped before O'Connell shook his head. 'We are going to have to request one.'

'That's going to build up their hopes.' Jenny's heart ached.

She knew handing over a DNA sample for a body which could be Melanie or Aunt Carolyn would have been torturous. But there was no doubt in her mind she would want to know if an unknown body was one of her family. The thought made her think of what Penny mentioned about checking evidence for her. She should ask her uncle for a DNA sample, just to exclude any unidentified bodies in the morgue.

O'Connell was watching her like he could read her thoughts, a sympathetic look crossed his features.

'I wish we had a choice, but we don't. If they never gave a DNA sample when she went missing, we'll need to ask for one now.' Sergeant Mackenzie rubbed his temples.

'If she's been missing for six years, someone has to have seen her around town. She would have outgrown her clothes years ago. She got new clothes somehow. Is there any reason to believe she willingly ran away from her parents?' Jenny stepped toward O'Connell, trying to see the file on the screen over his shoulder.

'I'll check.'

'Who took the Missing Person's Report? Where did she go missing?' Jenny was sure in the depths of her soul that her predecessor Senior Constable Len Holmes would likely be the signature on that report and if he was, would he be willing to cooperate in solving the girl's case?

'She went missing from a coach tour that travelled from Adelaide to Coober Pedy, then on to the William Creek Pub, William Creek Station, Dalhousie Springs before finishing up in Alice Springs.'

'What leg of the trip did they lose her on?' The pain in Jenny's stomach made her want to vomit. Penny stepped closer, a warm hand patted Jenny's back a few times before it stopped, leaving a fresh wave of discomfort. Penny and O'Connell were the only ones other than Nick who knew about her missing relatives. She wondered again if it was time to come clean with everyone else.

The wait while O'Connell tapped more keys and browsed files made Jenny's heart beat faster. She shoved her shaking hands into her pockets so no one would notice her anxiety, but Penny watched her closely.

'William Creek Pub. Apparently when the coach loaded in the morning, no one could find Beth.'

Jenny sat down hard, nearly toppling the chair next to O'Connell's desk. All eyes fell on her.

Chapter 11

'Are you okay?' Penny spoke softly, hoping not to be overheard.

Sergeant Mackenzie studied her, sitting with her head between her knees. 'What's up Williams?'

'Nothing Boss. Just a little lightheaded. Low blood-sugar.' She lied. 'Do you want me to take Penny out to the scene?'

Mackenzie scanned O'Connell's face for an answer. Was it to Jenny's questions or was he fishing for why she nearly collapsed next to O'Connell's desk?

'You two go. Take my Cruiser,' O'Connell answered. 'You good with driving on the wet mud?' Jenny nodded. 'Philips, call Mrs B. at the pub. Find out if she remembers the incident. I'll circulate a photo of the girl from the file. See if anyone knows anything in town.'

'I'll chat with Marj on the way out.' Jenny nodded to Penny. They hurried toward the door.

'Good idea, but don't let too much slip. You know what Marj can be like. She'll have a mob of locals all stirred up about a paedophile ring before we can blink,' Sarge called after them.

Jenny stopped by the door – a frown gave away the horrible thought that popped into her head. 'Have we run a victim profile through the database?'

'Don't even go there Williams!'

'Why not? You said it, not me. Remote bush locations are ideal for this type of ring to operate in.'

The Sergeant waved his hand, shooing her out the door. 'Let's just focus on the evidence for now.'

Jenny was about to argue, but O'Connell interrupted. 'I'll run a search Williams. Just to shut you up. Alright?'

Mackenzie huffed, turned on his heel and strode back to his office, slamming the door. She gave O'Connell a look between *thanks* and *what's his problem?* Before turning and leaving the station as frustrated as her Sergeant appeared to be.

'You really have to stop butting heads with him you know.' Penny offered as Jenny pressed the button to unlock the police vehicle.

She reached for the door handle, carefully avoiding the sticky red spray that covered most of the formerly white vehicle. A clump of thick, gloopy mud fell from the bottom of the door as she yanked it open.

'He always dismisses any sort of major crime. I don't get it.'

She slid in behind the wheel and turned the key as Penny closed the door and put her seatbelt on. A quick glance over her shoulder confirmed all the gear from earlier in the morning was still there. Jenny spun the wheels, a spray of mud flying through the air, the mudguards protesting with the impact.

'You come from a small town. You know how shocking gossip can be. I think your Sergeant doesn't like to get the rumour mill going, so he plugs any ideas you have quickly.' Jenny huffed as she parked outside the Motel Reception, avoiding the potholes in the bitumen carpark.

'I get the small-town gossip thing, but he doesn't have to shut *me* down. He can let the investigation run its course without blocking *me* at every turn.' Jenny pulled the keys from the ignition and got out. 'I follow up every lead, discretely. Besides, checking for other missing little girls isn't even going to pique on a local radar.'

'You'd be surprised.' Penny followed her into Reception to find Marj sitting behind the counter, watching a

US soap rerun that reminded Jenny of lunch time TV on the family farm.

'How's this wet Marj? Nuts.' The red-haired woman glanced up, a knowing smile crossing her face.

'I heard about the hit and run. Nasty. Do you know who the girl is yet?'

'Still figuring that out.' Jenny wasn't about to let the possible identity out right now. Her enquiry needed to be subtle. Marj could smell gossip a mile away.

'Where you headed today?'

'Out to the scene. We need to track down as much as we can before the mud settles.' Jenny pulled out her phone, opening a photo of the dead girl's face from the autopsy suite. 'Have you ever seen this girl in town? She's about seventeen and must have been living on a nearby station.'

'What makes you say that?' Marj studied Jenny's face, then her eyes fell on Penny. 'I thought it was an accident?'

'It was, but what we need to know is who to contact. Who do we tell, their daughter has died in a freak accident?' Jenny answered quickly. Penny averted her eyes from Marj's.

'So why is your forensic scientist still here?' The woman was too astute.

'Nothing gets by you does it Marj?' The woman studied the two girls. 'Can you take a look at the photo for me?' Jenny changed the subject, hoping to send the boisterous Motel owner on a new tangent, but no such luck.

'Was she murdered then?'

'No Marj. She was either lost in the bush, or she strayed from a nearby property. Her death was an accident. Do you know her?' Jenny wiggled the phone in front of Marj who watched Penny carefully before finally studying the face of the victim.

It was obvious Marj's red hair was no longer natural. Her pale brown eyebrows bent in the middle as she studied the photo carefully. 'Oh the poor little thing. It's pretty hard to tell from this photo. All the life is gone...'

'Is there anything that sparks your memory? Was she with a tour group maybe?' Jenny knew she was clutching at straws. If the tour stayed at Marj's Motel, it would have been years ago. The girl would have been younger, her face more immature. The likelihood of anyone remembering her then would be slim, but maybe they saw her around town more recently.

Or maybe they were barking up the wrong tree and their victim wasn't the missing girl at all. She might have stolen or picked up Beth's necklace.

Marj shook her head in the negative. Jenny moved to put her phone away, but Marj grabbed her hand and stopped her.

'What is it?'

'That necklace.' Marj's brow was even more creased now, if that were even possible. 'I've seen it before, but I can't for the life of me think where.'

Jenny glanced over to Penny who shrugged that this part of police work wasn't exactly her area of expertise.

'It's okay Marj. Let it sink in. It will come to you. We've got work to do but if you think of anything, anything even a small, insignificant thing, just give me a call.'

'Will do, but you have to let me know if this is a murder or not?'

'It's not a murder Marj.' *Was it murder?* Even though the truck driver didn't hit the girl on purpose, whoever left her out there alone was responsible for her death. This girl went missing six years ago. Now she was dead. Someone was going to have to answer for that.

Chapter 12

The vehicle slid from side to side. A clump of mud flew onto the windscreen. Jenny flicked the wipers on, pressing the water button as the wipers groaned against the thick goo. The windscreen began to clear. She hit the water on the wipers again. Nothing.

'Damn. I'm out of water.' The vehicle jumped and rocked some more. 'Have you seen the Crash Investigation Report yet?' Jenny's brow was furrowed, her hands sweaty as she kept her focus on what was left of the road. Rivers of thick mud floated on the rough surface, making it difficult to pick a clean line or stay in the vehicle tracks already forged by trucks.

'No. I'll check when we get back. Hopefully the preliminary report on the girl is back by then too. I'm keen to see what we got from her fingernails. Doc Holbrook put her on the top of his list when I explained the strange circumstances of her discovery.'

'No shoes. Her feet were torn up. How far do you think she managed to run like that?'

'With the sharp, shale type rock out here,' Penny shrugged, barely seen by Jenny as her eyes stayed fixed on the terrain, 'who knows? She might have only gone a kilometre or so. If her feet were soft, on this stuff, she'd be cut to ribbons in no time.'

A taped off area on the side of the road showed what was left of the accident scene. They donned rubber boots before stepping out of the vehicle. Jenny watched as Penny slowly rotated to take in the desolate landscape.

'There's nothing out here but bush, rock and the occasional mound of dirt.'

'Makes you wonder where she came from, hey.'

'That's for sure. Did you check the maps? Is there anything out here?' Penny opened the rear doors of the Landcruiser and retrieved her forensic kit.

'There are a few stations. A couple of large iron-ore mines south of here, but there's not many places where a young woman would be living.'

'The rain is going to have done a lot of damage. I'm not sure what I'll be able to find, but let's see if anything managed to *not* get washed away or buried in the mud. Then we can organise a search team.'

'Sarge said we were expecting a tracker.'

'Well he's obviously not here yet. I want to get started here anyway.' Penny handed Jenny a pair of gloves before closing her case and shutting the back door of the police vehicle. Jenny pressed the lock button and the lights blinked as they approached the taped off area.

Amazingly, the hastily erected tent withstood the pouring rain and wind, protecting the scene as much as possible under the circumstances. Jenny scanned the area for any sign of blood, but there was nothing left to signify the state she found the victim in when she arrived Friday.

Crusted mud layered the surface, but collapsed as soon as her boot touched down, sucking her feet into the wet earth. Each step was hard work, as the mud tried to pull her boot from her foot, then stuck to it, making each step heavier than the last.

'Hey, look at this.' Jenny leant down over a broken piece of vehicle.

Penny followed Jenny's tracks, taking slow and deliberate steps to avoid slipping in the mud. She carried a small bundle of evidence bags, along with a permanent marker. 'The crash investigation team likely collected what they needed as far as vehicle bits.'

'Maybe, but does this look like it came from the truck to you?' Jenny pointed to a four-wheel drive hub cap that was too small to have come from a bigrig. 'And these tracks look fresh.' Jenny pointed to a deep tyre track that ran up the edge of the road, onto the rocky ground around their crash site.

'Someone has been out this morning after the crash team finished up.' Penny opened an evidence bag and lifted the hub cap with her stainless-steel pointer, before dropping it into the bag.

'Look. These are boot prints.' Jenny followed two sets of prints to the taped off site. Both went beyond the tape making the young constable's blood boil. 'Whoever they are, they tromped all over the scene.'

'At least their tracks are obvious. I'll know where they've been. Let's see what we can find.' Penny sealed the bag and ducked under the tape.

A noise, growing slowly louder made them turn in unison. Jenny gazed up, the sound of the chopper unmistakable as she recalled the day Nick and she rode out on horseback at the William Creek Station to see Ed and Al.

The small cattle mustering helicopter dropped low over the scene, flying onward, away before landing in the rocky, barren field beyond.

'Looks like our tracker might have arrived.' Penny nodded as an elderly indigenous man, with grey hair and a worn out Akubra hat jumped nimbly to the ground.

'That's Al, from William Creek Station.'

Penny grinned as a tall, broad man jumped out of the pilot's seat, pulling on his Akubra before strolling over to join Al. 'I take it that's Nick then?'

Jenny considered her friend's stupid grin, then punched her lightly on the arm. 'Not a word.'

Penny zipped her lips and turned the key, but the grin returned too fast. A feeling of nausea swept through Jenny's stomach. Penny often opened her big mouth at the worst possible time, and now showed all the ear marks of one of those moments.

The whirring of the chopper blades slowed then stopped as Nick and his tracker crossed the rocky terrain.

'Your boss said you needed a tracker? Is someone lost?' Nick stepped closer. 'You remember Al?'

'Sure. Thanks for coming. No one is lost, but a girl was hit by a truck here Friday.' Nick surveyed the terrain, ready to state the obvious. 'We know. There's no car here and no houses nearby. That's why we need a tracker.' Jenny's gaze fell on Al.

He relit the smoke dangling from his lip, but held back, listening and watching, saying nothing.

'It's going to be tricky after all this rain.' Nick glanced at Al, who grunted, his smoke finally lit up, he sucked in and puffed a few times to make sure it stuck.

'Don't we know it. Half our evidence is likely stuck in the mud or trampled by all these footprints.' Penny waved her arm, drawing Nick's attention to the churned-up earth all around the tent and taped off area.

'We have reason to believe this young woman wasn't out here by choice.' Jenny watched Al and Nick closely. There was still something in the back of her mind that kept niggling at her. *Did Nick know what happened to her cousin and aunt. Was he keeping something from her?*

If Nick knew anything, he was damn good at hiding it.

'Are you saying she was abducted and dumped out here?' Nick frowned, the look of concern made his crystal blue eyes darken.

'We don't know.' Jenny decided less was best. She kept the specifics to herself. 'She could have hitched out here and someone got too touchy or maybe she was working on a station nearby and got lost.' She didn't mention the girl was found without any shoes and was likely abducted six years ago.

'Al and I will see what we can find.'

'Thanks. We could do with the help.' Jenny turned, but stopped as she remembered the hub cap in the plastic evidence bag. 'Do you know what vehicle this might be from?' She pointed and Nick followed her finger to the bag Penny now waved in the air like a magician's assistant.

'It's pretty generic. Landcruiser, Nissan. He studied it more closely. 'Actually, it looks pretty heavy duty. I'd say one of the mining vehicles from down south… Bunker Hill way.' Al nodded agreement with his boss before turning to study the ground, his smoke dead on his lip again.

'Do you want us to track the car or the girl?' Nick waited patiently for a reply.

'The car tracks are probably just hoons out to check out why we've got crime scene tape up, but if something looks out of whack, let me know. Otherwise, we'll stick to finding where the girl might have come from. Thanks.'

Chapter 13

Jenny wiped the sweat from her forehead before unscrewing the top of her drink bottle. Taking a long, slow swig of cool water did nothing to reduce the heat building up inside her core like a firecracker.

Sweat beaded and ran down her back. Putting the top back on her drink bottle, she barely resisted the urge to pour some over her head first. Water was scarce, even after all this rain. The sun pelted down, doing its best to dry out the mud. Humidity was high, leaving every inch of her khaki police uniform wet, sticky and stuck to her skin like maple syrup.

They spent the best part of the morning poking around in the semi-dry mud, looking for anything that would help them discover where the girl came from before being struck by the road train that killed her.

'I'll need to come back when this dirt is dry and do a proper job of sifting it but look at this. At least we found something.' Penny held up a piece of torn fabric.

'Purple and red. She definitely wasn't wearing anything that colour.' Jenny stepped closer, under the pop-up marquee still on site.

'And its newer than her clothing. Look, there's no sign of fading.' Penny reached inside her pocket for an evidence bag.

'What do you think it's from?'

'No idea.' Penny placed it in a bag. Using a permanent marker to label it, she turned to put it into a cardboard box of evidence. The single piece of fabric was all that occupied the box. Penny glanced up, then nodded over Jenny's shoulder before continuing to scour the ground for more evidence.

'It gets a bit muggy out here after heavy rain.' Jenny turned in time to see Nick swing his canteen around his neck. His shirt stuck to his chest, revealing every muscle in detail.

Jenny forced herself to make eye contact. 'It's pretty unpleasant, but we're coping. Did you find anything?'

'Not a lot. The tyre tracks went south, like we thought, over the land that way. All the property this side of the road is government lease, operated by the big iron-ore mining firms.'

'So the tracks were made *after* the rain stopped?' Jenny glanced over to Al for clarification.

'Yep Miss.' His white teeth smiled momentarily, then disappeared as his unlit rollie nearly slipped free of his grey moustached lip.

'Anything of our girl?' Jenny wasn't expecting much. The road was lower than the surrounding land where the victim was found. When they left Friday, there was a river flowing from high to low ground, likely taking any evidence with it into the muddy road.

'Nah.' Al was a man of few words it seemed.

'We couldn't read any tracks. The rain did a number on everything and there's very little saltbush or brush out here to indicate which direction she came from. We don't know how she got out here Constable.'

Jenny squirmed at her formal title. She and Nick weren't exactly best buddies, but they spent a few hours together trying to figure out what happened to her aunt and cousin. She also offered to help dig up information about his dad's supposed suicide. Why was he being so curt?

'That's a little formal isn't it?' Penny's big mouth opened and Jenny found herself wishing the earth would swallow her up. Thankful her blush was hidden by her already flushed face.

'Just being respectful to the local authorities Miss.'

'Penny. Call me Penny.' Nick hesitated a moment, then nodded as Penny continued un-phased. 'We don't know how she got out here either. Any ideas what's close enough to get to on foot?'

'This spot is miles from anywhere.'

'Where are the closest stations? Are there *any* close by? I'd like to interview the owners?' Jenny got her phone from her pants pocket, her utility vest was too hot, so she removed it earlier. Not strictly protocol, but no one could possibly sneak up on her today.

'Close by is an oxymoron out here. This area is barren, with little feed except after a wet spell. There are a few stations in the vicinity, but each station is literally tens of thousands of square kilometres.'

'Whose station are we on now then?'

Nick regarded his surroundings, got his bearings, then drew a slow steady breath, his top lip curled and his nostrils flared slightly as he gauged the location.

'We are about half way to William Creek Pub. I'd say we are right on the border of Rocky Neville and Kent Murphy's place.'

Al grunted he agreed and returned to trying to reignite his dead smoke by sucking on it hard. Unsuccessful, he began rummaging in his pocket for a lighter or match.

'Do you know much about them?'

Nick shrugged. 'Both own about twenty square kilometres of land. Run cattle much like we do at William Creek Station.'

'They have a few farm hands then?' Jenny waited, her phone ready to take notes.

'I expect they have a permanent staff of about ten or fifteen, with shearers and drovers coming and going during the season. A few backpackers to help out here and there.'

57

'Backpackers. Are they much help?' Penny glanced over from her evidence hunt.

'A bit. Most of them are next to useless, but a few are good help in the kitchen or doing basic things like cleaning the workers' quarters. Occasionally you find one who's worked on farms before.'

'You finished up here Penny?' Jenny checked over her shoulder to see Penny writing on a zip lock bag, a sample of dirt inside.

'Almost done for now. I'll need to come back when it's dryer, but I'll chat with the crash team first, confirm they haven't picked up anything I'll need to go over.'

'You okay if on the way back we call in on the properties Nick mentioned?'

'Lunch will have to wait I guess.' Penny started packing her bags up.

'Longer than you might think.' Nick offered. 'The entrance to Murphy's homestead is another twenty-five minutes towards William Creek Pub and then you'll need to head halfway to my place on the Oodnadatta track before you find the entrance to Neville's homestead.'

'Damn.' Jenny sighed.

'I could drop Al back and give you a lift in the chopper if you like,' Nick peered over at Penny, 'but I don't have room for two of you.'

Jenny shook her head but Penny interrupted. 'I can drive myself back.' Her top lip curled with a suspicious grin.

As much as Jenny wanted an excuse to spend some time going over her family case with Nick, that wasn't a workable solution.

'I wouldn't have any way of getting back into town afterwards.'

'I can drive you in. I've got some supplies to collect in any case.' Nick offered and Penny's eyebrows rose in a way that said *You're out of excuses Honey!*

'Are you sure?'

'I'm sure. Give me twenty minutes.' Nick ushered Al back into the chopper. Jenny watched, stunned as the blades began to whir into life. The helicopter disappeared. She continued to stare out over the horizon, her mind racing with questions. A voice made her jump.

Penny laughed. 'Didn't mean to startle you. I thought you said he was aloof?'

Jenny couldn't speak. The fact that Nick was going out of his way to help her was shocking, wonderful, but still shocking.

'He usually is.' She finally found her voice.

'Not today.'

Chapter 14

Jenny's stomach lurched as the fast, manoeuvrable chopper took flight. She stifled a giggle, but as she glanced over at Nick, she could see him smiling.

'It's a buzz, especially your first time.'

'It's like a roller coaster ride.' Jenny adjusted the microphone on the earphones Nick gave her. 'These are handy.'

Nick nodded. 'It's impossible to talk over the sound of this little bugger otherwise.'

'When did you learn to fly?' She studied his profile as he kept his eyes out the dome-shaped windscreen. His cheekbones were sharp, his nose long, but sleek.

'Around the same time as I learnt to drive. About ten.' He glanced at her, his expression serious once more.

'We had bikes, tractors and utes when I was a kid. I would have loved to learn to fly one of these.'

'I'll give you a lesson.'

She didn't expect him to be so warm and inviting. The only other time she recalled him so casual was when he took her to see the aboriginal paintings on the escarpment at his station. The memory made her skin tingle and it wasn't only because of the spiritual energy the cave paintings exuded.

'Tempting. Another time maybe. I wouldn't want to crash your little bird while I'm in uniform.' Nick studied her khakis a moment and nodded. His eyes focussed back outside of the helicopter. Her stomach knotted with the sudden mood swing.

'Nearly at Kent's place.' Nick pointed down as they passed over a new fence line leading to a set of cattle yards nestled amongst a stand of mature gum trees. A water trough sat alone in the paddock. 'That's his place over there.' Nick pointed. Jenny followed his finger to find a long, stone homestead surrounded by tin sheds, not unlike Nick's family home.

The chopper began to lower over a large circle of well-kept, cleanly mowed grass. 'Hang onto your hat as you get out and keep your head low.'

Nick pulled his earphones off and Jenny did the same, placing them carefully on her seat as she jumped from the small helicopter. There were no doors to prevent her from an easy and quick exit. Her skin tingled as she felt the powerful airflow overhead. Holding her hat tightly, she jogged away from the blades' radius.

What was probably everyday boring for Nick made Jenny's adrenalin fire. Her heart raced with excitement.

Steadying herself, she strode over the grass, then tiptoed over the still muddy circular driveway leading to the front porch steps. To the left of the main entrance, a set of French doors sat open wide. Outside, looking bored, a short round man in his mid to late fifties watched her approach. He waited, his thumbs hooked in his empty belt buckles.

Jenny pulled her hat off as she climbed the stairs but waited for Nick before approaching the stoic looking farmer.

'Mr Murphy. I'm Constable Williams, from Coober Pedy.'

The man reached for her offered hand and nodded as Nick drew up alongside. 'Nicholas.' The tone wasn't impolite, but there was something in it that made Jenny watch them carefully. They barely made eye contact. Nick hovered back, both hands in his pockets.

'Kent.' Nick shook the offered hand, then stuffed it back in his pocket, his whole body was rigid.

Jenny didn't have time to consider the weird body language. She needed to focus on her job. 'Mr Murphy. There was an accident on or near your property Friday.'

'Heard about it.' Jenny could smell her own BO. Mr Murphy didn't seem the least bit phased by it.

'I've got a photo of the woman who was killed. Can I show it to you? I'm afraid we only have the morgue photo?' Jenny wished for a more recent one, but she couldn't use the photos from Beth's file because they were all of her as a child. Faces changed dramatically from pre-teens to adult and they still didn't have a formal ID.

'I'm not squeamish luv. You can show me but I don't know any girls nearby that have gone missing.'

'Maybe you've seen her around then? With one of your workers possibly?'

Jenny retrieved her phone from her utility vest. She preferred not to be wearing her Kevlar vest, but it was mandatory when on official police business.

'Take your time. It can be hard to recognise someone you don't know well from a morgue photo.'

She knew a morgue photo often didn't resemble the living person. The colour of the skin was beyond white, almost translucent. Lividity caused strange bruising under the skin and the lips were often bluish, purple which changed the overall appearance of how a person appeared in life.

She turned her phone to face the farmer. He peered intently a moment.

'Mr Murphy. I'm just…' A woman came around the corner of the homestead and stopped when she realised she was interrupting. Her accent wasn't local but Jenny wanted as many eyes on this photo as she could get.

'Anna. Can't you see I'm busy.'

'Sorry.' She turned to leave.

'Actually. Maybe you can help me?' Jenny eyeballed the woman, who averted her gaze.

'Anna doesn't know anything.' Mr Murphy tried to shoo the woman away, but Jenny interrupted.

'I don't mean to be rude Sir. I'm new around here, but I think I can still work out what might be helpful or not to our investigation.'

'You said yourself it was an accident.' The words were rushed. Jenny studied the man, whose eyes darted to Anna. The woman appeared ready to run for cover.

'The truck hitting the woman was an accident Sir. Why she was out in the middle of nowhere is what we are investigating.' Jenny approached the new arrival. 'Anna, right?' The woman nodded. 'Can you look at this photo for me please? Maybe this woman worked here, or dated one of the workers?'

Jenny stepped closer, but stopped as the smell of the woman's clothing reached her nostrils. There was no mistaking the scent. Jenny suddenly understood the woman's elusive behaviour.

'Have you seen her?' Jenny showed the photo on her phone. Anna pushed her nerves aside to study the photo. Her squinted eyes focussed. Jenny watched her closely. Finally, she shook her head.

'I'm sorry.' Her accent sounded Scandinavian, German maybe.

'That's okay. So, you've not seen her around here at all?' Another shake of the head. 'Thanks for trying.' Jenny returned to Mr Murphy. The tension in Anna's body relaxed. 'Maybe you can take a closer look now too.'

'I took a look. I've never seen her before and we've got work to do.' Jenny breathed a sigh and turned to Nick who was standing right where she left him, leaning against a veranda post, trying to appear relaxed. Jenny could see he wasn't. The muscle on the side of his jaw twitched, it was a tell she picked up the moment she met him.

'Can I speak with your workers?'

'Look, they are all busy. We don't have overnight guests here, only staff and if I've never seen her and Anna has never seen her, then she's never been here.'

'Anna.' Jenny turned back to the woman. 'What's your role here?'

Anna's eyes darted to Mr Murphy's seeking permission to answer the question. The act made Jenny's skin crawl. 'Where are you from?' She pushed for an answer.

'I think you can go now Constable. I'll be having a chat with Sergeant Mackenzie next time I'm in town.'

'You should do that Sir. I certainly will be. Maybe you can give *him* a straight answer.' Jenny didn't wait for a reply. She spun on her heel, shoved her hat back on her head a little hard and tried desperately not to stomp her feet as she stalked down the concrete veranda to the stairs where Nick waited.

He followed her to the chopper without a word. She was certain he overheard her conversation. Thoughts were jumping around her head as she picked up the earphones and placed them over her ears and buckled her seatbelt.

Nick got in alongside and started the chopper motor before putting his own earphones on. 'Get anything useful.'

'Only more questions I'm afraid.' The chopper lifted off. Jenny stared at the two people on the veranda, holding their hats and staring just as hard back at her.

Chapter 15

Jenny could feel Nick's eyes studying her as they flew toward William Creek Station. While Kent Murphy made her suspicious, she wasn't sure he was involved in what happened to her victim.

On the other hand, Rocky Neville struck her as a true country gentleman. The station owner was in his seventies with no sons or grandsons to take over his property. She wouldn't totally rule him out yet, but nothing about the man or his property set off alarm bells.

But her instincts weren't always to be trusted. The silence was tense. Maybe Nick didn't know what to say? She needed to change the subject.

'I've downloaded your dad's file.' Nick glanced her way, but said nothing. 'I've been too busy to study it, but I wanted you to know I've not forgotten.'

The aloof Nick was back. Why? The glare that passed between him and Murphy popped into her head. 'What's your history with Mr Murphy?'

Maybe that was a worse subject than his dad's death? Nick's lips pulled tightly together. It seemed nothing she said was a good subject, but at least he didn't stay quiet this time.

'That obvious.'

'Pretty obvious to a trained investigator like myself.' She smiled as she puffed on her knuckles and rubbed them on her collar for added emphasis.

Nick laughed, something he rarely did. She liked it. The fine creases around his eyes said it didn't happen often enough.

'Murphy's wife left him about fifteen years ago. A few years after their only son was born.' Jenny waited. That wasn't a reason to dislike the guy. 'There was talk of an affair.'

Nick didn't look at her. His eyes remained focussed outside the curved chopper window as the ochre and sandstone coloured earth passed beneath them. She knew what he was thinking, but remained quiet.

'He was always too touchy feely with mum. I'm not saying anything ever happened, but the guy is a sleaze.'

'Do you know anything about Anna?' The idea that a sleazy guy was holding something over an international student or backpacker wasn't a calming thought.

'Nope. Never met her before.'

Jenny put the woman's face into her memory bank, deciding she needed to do some more digging when she got the chance. They flew over a small stand of gumtrees that were out of place amongst the large expanse of nothingness below. Jenny kept her eyes on the rundown shack and cattle yards as the chopper passed by.

'Who owns the property below us?'

Nick was now focussed on the sky and terrain, but he knew exactly where they were. 'The edge of Murphy's property, where it borders the Oodnadatta Track.' He studied her again, his intense blue gaze causing his brows to furrow and Jenny's heart to skip a beat.

Shaking free of his gaze, she refocussed on her job. Nick was her means to discovering what happened to her cousin and aunt, that and to help with this investigation. Going all gooey over a guy was not on her agenda.

'I saw a run-down shed down there.' Nick responded to the question in her voice instantly. Without a word or even a gaze in her direction, he circled the little Robinson R22 chopper back around, making her a little giddy.

'Looks like a watering point for cattle.' Nick explained as they circled around for another pass.

'What direction is this place in relation to where we found the girl's body?'

'North-east. Why?'

'How many kilometres away?' Jenny kept her eye on the building. The tin and wood construction was weathered. The roofing iron was lifting in one corner, the wooden palings discoloured and worn.

'You think she might have been held out here?' Nick circled around once more as the hairs on the back of her neck rose.

'Can we take a look inside?' Nick didn't answer, instead he began manoeuvring the helicopter in what felt like a sideways fashion towards a clearing.

'You're pretty good at this.' Nick gave her another rare smile but returned his focus to landing the chopper on a rocky, uneven patch of ground.

'I'll come with you.' Nick powered down the chopper and removed his earphones.

'I'm okay!' Jenny removed her earphones and hung them over the hook by the doorway. She was finding her way around the chopper now.

'I'm not taking no for an answer.' Nick slipped from the pilot's seat before she could argue.

I'm the one carrying the gun! She huffed to herself as she jumped out, the chopper blades winding down above her.

Don't mistake chivalry for chauvinism. Philips' words reminded her that guys just wanted to protect. It was in their DNA. It didn't mean they thought she was weak, well most of the time it didn't.

'Okay, but can I take the lead?' She patted her pistol hoping it would explain but Nick didn't seem convinced. 'This is a police matter, so I'll get hauled over the coals if someone opens fire and hits you, not me first.' She tapped her bulletproof vest. 'I'm dressed for it.'

Nick reluctantly pulled back, waiting for her to step in front as they cautiously passed the fallen wooden railing on the once functioning stock yard.

'The trough is empty, so there aren't any cattle grazing this paddock right now.' Nick offered as Jenny tried to get her bearings.

'They can't be using these yards now either.' She pointed to a rusted cattle crush and another broken rail before continuing watchfully toward the dishevelled shack.

'Hang on.' Nick whispered, then pointed to something alongside the shed. Blow flies swarmed over a compact mound of dirt.

Jenny's skin tingled, the hairs on the back of her neck stood to attention. Unclipping her pistol, she pulled her Taser free of the clip. Holding it in her left hand, she advanced cautiously toward the mound of black flies.

'It looks like…' Jenny stopped, turned her head away and gagged as the smell of rotting flesh wafted towards them. She held her breath and carried on, until Nick stopped her, a hand on her shoulder.

'I don't think that's a dead animal Jenny.' It was the first time he used her name all day. That and something in his voice made her stop her advance. Looking past the black blanket of flies she saw a piece of fabric. Her blood ran cold.

'I'm going to have to call Penny out here.'

'I think you should, but it looks like the wildlife have already taken their fill. Your phone won't work out here. I'll use the chopper radio.'

'Hang on. I need to clear the area first.' Jenny turned to carry on her primary route to the shed. With her Taser still at the ready, she opened the door. The metal hinge creaked eerily, the sound vibrating down Jenny's spine. One look inside made her stomach heave.

'We need to get that call out. Now!'

Chapter 16

The sky was streaked with white, rainless clouds. The colours of the sunset would have been spectacular if it weren't for the gruesome surroundings. Jenny observed Penny as the forensic scientist shot photos of what was left of an infant's body. As if the child's death wasn't horrific enough, it paled against the state of the bloody mattress and stained walls inside the shed.

'When did she go missing?' Nick remained on scene, and waited with Jenny while nearly every team in the Coober Pedy police station ventured out to the edge of Murphy's station.

'I'm sorry. I can't go into details.' Nick didn't seem offended by her keeping the information close to her chest, but part of her wanted to tell him what she knew. Part of her needed to offload all the foul details of this case.

Penny delicately unearthed the remains, wrapped lovingly in pale purple and red linen swaddling. The shallow grave was fresh, the body too close to the surface not to be found and dug up by local wildlife.

'I think this will match the fabric we found on our victim, but we'll need to analyse it to be sure. The baby could be premature judging by the size of the femur, but I'm not the expert on that. I'll update Doc Holbrook and see if he can confirm the baby was hers, the gestational period and cause of death. This fabric might help.' Penny added the infant blanket to another evidence bag.

'We've got a lot of evidence to collect here. Thanks for your help today Nick. I couldn't have gotten around to station owners without you, but you should probably head back before it gets dark.'

Nick wasn't in a hurry to move. She knew he understood choppers like his only flew by sight. The light was fading fast and he was still a fair way from William Creek Station.

'Okay, but if you or your team need a chopper again, you let me know. Okay? Everything out here is a long way between stops and something like this, happening close to home, just leaves a bad taste in my mouth.'

Jenny thought about her aunt and cousin going missing and how that happened close to Nick's home but stayed silent. This case was raw. His reaction was expected. Nick's eyes lingered, following her hand as she massaged the tension in her neck.

'Thanks. I'll let you know if we need help, but today has answered a lot of questions.' *And brought up a lot of new ones.*

Nick returned to the chopper, stopping a moment. He turned back, as though he wanted to say something, but she saw him shake his head, changing his mind. She watched as he jumped into the pilot's seat and pressed the button to get the engine going.

Her thoughts drifted to how the day had started out so well and ended so horribly.

'Williams.' Jenny turned to see Sergeant Mackenzie standing behind her, near the disused water trough, his arms crossed over his chest.

'On my way Sir.' She jogged over to the shed to continue helping Penny collect evidence.

'I'll leave you with McGregor and Philips to finish up here. I think I'll go interview Murphy again on the way home.'

Jenny wanted to protest but she knew it was futile. 'If you think that's best Sir.' The words slipped out before she could stop herself.

'What is that supposed to mean Williams?'

'Sir, I questioned Murphy this morning. He was less than helpful. In fact, he basically said he was going to be reporting me to you. Maybe he'll be more open with a local.'

His mouth opened to speak, then closed. She didn't want to challenge his authority. She just wanted him to consider how close he was to Murphy. His blinkers needed to come off.

'I'll keep an open mind Williams.'

'Yes Sir.' Jenny continued past her commanding officer toward the shed.

Plywood covered what should have been windows, ensuring prying eyes wouldn't get a quick look. Inside was dark, but the beam of light from the open door was enough to tell Jenny that this was the victim's prison.

The two-inch-thick mattress was threadbare and covered in blood. The dirt floor smelled of urine. Jenny's eyes fell on the chain and collar attached to a rough sawn wooden post in the corner. Her stomach clenched.

'Did she escape from that?' Jenny pointed. Penny carried on dusting for prints. Philips' expression in the artificial spotlights was haunted. 'You can get some air if you want mate. I'll help Penny.'

Without hesitation, Philips ducked his head through the low door opening, taking a deep breath on the way out.

'Nasty.' Jenny leant over Penny and adjusted the flood light for the forensic scientist.

'I've seen worse.'

'In that case, I'm bloody glad I don't have your job. Should we be calling in a detective?'

'I'd say yes, but you and I both know the Sergeant isn't likely to oblige. I'll need to get some more evidence before we can be sure this is where Elizabeth Thompson was being kept.'

'That's if our victim *is* Beth Thompson.'

'I'll DNA match this blood. I'll also do a DNA match on the deceased child.'

'That could take months.'

'I'll rush it, but yes, it could take a while.' Penny tore a piece of tape from the collar of the chain, placed it on a card and pressed down firmly.

'Can we at least tell the parents?'

'That will be up to your Sergeant, but we need DNA and that's the only way we'll get it. I got the report back on the victim's body this afternoon, before you called this in.'

'And?'

Penny used stainless steel scissors to cut a tiny, neat square of the mattress fabric away. She placed it in an evidence bag as she spoke.

'Her body was riddled with broken bones. All healed except the most recent, from the crash. It appeared none was professionally set though.

'You think she's been a prisoner, here, for six years?'

'She's been a sex slave to a paedophile is what I think she's been.'

'But paedophiles don't like them older. Why keep her? Why not just kill her?'

'And that's the million-dollar question isn't it.' Penny collated her samples and rose to continue assessing the scene with a flashlight.

'And if you are going to keep her, for someone to play with—and whoever did this must have let someone play with her for her to get pregnant...'

'Assuming the baby is hers.'

'There is that, but the swaddling fabric is a strong connection and if it's her baby, why didn't anyone put her on the pill or use protection?'

'A guy getting the pill without taking her into town?' Penny opened another evidence bag and placed a hair inside.'

'Good point. But that means it's not likely a professional job. They can get the pill easily enough. If he's local, small time, why didn't he try to palm her off to the town doctor as his sister, or daughter?'

'He was worried someone would know him, and it's a long way between towns out here to try a different doctor.'

'I wonder if he tried any of the aboriginal community clinics?'

'That would be worth a try.'

'I hope Sarge gets somewhere with Murphy because I find it hard to believe he didn't know someone was keeping a sex slave on his property. Or maybe his international worker knows something.'

Chapter 17

Jenny rushed around the small kitchen, a piece of toast and peanut butter in her mouth.

There were advantages to living in a dugout. The main one being the lack of sunlight made sleeping in easy – the negative – the lack of sunlight made sleeping in easy.

They worked well into the night, collecting evidence. Philips drove them home after ten, but Jenny wasn't going to bed without a shower. It was well after one a.m. when she finally fell into bed.

Nev and Tim were on the early shifts, leaving the house deadly quiet. On any other day that would have been awesome, but no morning noise, no sunlight, no alarm because she forgot to set it meant Jenny was now searching for Nev's keys.

Sarge wasn't going to be happy she was running late. But the worst part was Jenny wouldn't be able to stop off and grab a coffee on the way.

Ten minutes later, she glanced at her watch as she parked outside the station. Throwing the door open, she undid her belt, grabbed her bag and lunged forward to get out. The seatbelt jerked her backwards, nearly ripping her arm out of the socket.

'Damn!' She slammed the door, rubbed her shoulder and jogged inside.

Philips looked like she felt. He still mustered up the energy to find a grin as she lifted the counter-top, carefully lowering in the hopes of not being spotted coming in late. Placing her bag in her locker, she glanced to the back of the building fully expecting Sergeant MacKenzie to yell her name out at any moment. When nothing happened, she let out a slow breath, then approached O'Connell at his desk.

'Sarge not in yet?'

'No. He's later than you.' O'Connell grinned, making it clear he was aware how long everyone spent digging up evidence. 'Penny should be here in a minute. Called to say she was making a few stops before dropping in to brief us.'

'Okay. I'll get to writing up my report then.' She crossed to the main office computer on the counter.

'Good idea, but how about a quick recap for me before you do that?'

'Maybe we can do it all together with Penny, if that's okay? I'm not fully awake yet.' She returned to O'Connell's desk, put her hand up around her mouth blocking Philips' view and whispered. 'I'm not relishing the office coffee. I missed my early morning pick me up.' He smiled, then lifted his chin toward the door as Penny arrived.

'Hope I got the orders right.' Penny held out a cardboard tray loaded with coffee cups. Jenny almost sighed aloud as the aroma of real beans hit her senses. 'Carmel syrup, right!'

'You-are-a-*lifesaver.*' Jenny's voice rang out like a singsong on the last word. She reached for the coffee, retrieving it from Penny's hand, pulled it to her lips, inhaling deeply.

Noticing a heavy forensic bag in Penny's free hand, a cardboard tray of undelivered coffees in the other, she stopped herself before taking a sip.

'Here, let me get that for you.' Jenny used her free hand to grab the bag while Penny handed out the rest of the coffees.

'Okay. Doc Holbrook has been able to confirm that our victim has given birth recently. We'll know if she is indeed Elizabeth Thompson later today with a rush on DNA now the Thompson's have arrived in Adelaide. Doc has confirmed her pelvic bones have a widening, there is a tear in her perineum and debris was found in her uterus from what looks like a very difficult birth.'

'The poor kid. Out there all alone, giving birth.' Jenny sat down on the corner of O'Connell's desk. Philips' already pale complexion went ghostly.

'We don't know she was alone.' O'Connell said before taking a long sip of his coffee. 'Okay kids. Where are we at?'

'I interviewed both station owners yesterday. Murphy has an international assistant of some sort working for him. She was cagey but then I smelt dope on her, which could explain her behaviour. Either way, Murphy set off alarm bells for me. Now we've found the girl's empty prison on the edge of his property, maybe I rattled his cage?'

'Maybe.' O'Connell didn't look convinced. Did he know Murphy? 'Did Nick put up any resistance to landing by the shed?'

Jenny was surprised Nick's name came up in discussion. The Senior Constable always spoke highly of the guy. Could he seriously be a suspect?

'Not at all. He wanted to go first to begin with, but I insisted I had the gun, the Taser and the badge.'

'It was Nick who offered to take Jenny out to interview the station owners.' Penny pointed out. O'Connell nodded before taking another drink of his coffee.

'We found the baby's body first.'

'What made you think it was a child's body?'

'We didn't at first. It was Nick who knew it wasn't an animal. I guess he's seen a few dead dingos and possums in his time.'

'Then what?'

'Then I opened the shed and saw the blood on the mattress. I was fairly certain this was where the girl was held.'

'Okay, Sarge has re-interviewed Murphy while you and Penny were busy at the scene.'

'Great, has he sent in his report yet?'

'No. He phoned to say he wouldn't be in until late today.'

Jenny wanted to push, but she was too far down the food chain to even consider asking questions about her boss' movements. There would have been a time she would have assumed Sergeant Mackenzie wasn't on the up and up, but she knew him now and despite his unwillingness to allow a detective in on the case and his need to keep everything local, he was a good cop who just wanted to protect his town.

'Blood type on the mattress is a match for our victim. I'd say once we get the DNA check pushed up the ladder we'll confirm the baby is hers too. The swaddling fabric is a match to the piece found on the victim, but that's still circumstantial.'

'Do we call in a detective from Adelaide or Alice?' Jenny was surprised to hear the words she wanted to say come out of Philips' mouth.

'This case has been flagged in Adelaide. If the DNA is a match to Beth Thompson, I think we'll see a detective on our doorstep shortly afterward. The Thompsons will likely insist on it.'

'So what do you need us to do today Sir?' Jenny waited on O'Connell for instructions.

'Sounds like we've got everything we can get from the accident site for now.' He deferred to Penny who nodded confirmation.

Penny started packing up her equipment. 'I'll be heading back to Adelaide this afternoon. I've got a lot of evidence to run through testing now and I prefer to oversee it personally.'

'Thanks Penny.' Jenny wished her friend could stay. Her company made for a great weekend, but now they needed to get back to work. 'Sorry to see you head back but I'm keen to find out what we can about who abducted Elizabeth Thompson all those years ago.'

'Me too.'

'Philips, you and Williams head out to the mine and see if you can find out why one of their vehicles was hooning around our police accident site. You should be able to find which vehicle was out that way by the missing hub cap, but if not, ask for their vehicle logs and see if you can narrow it down. Why were they out there? What were they looking for? Just a joy ride or are they linked to our victim somehow?'

'On it Sir.' Jenny gave O'Connell a quick salute and opened her locker to retrieve her utility vest. She sculled the last of her coffee before turning to Penny.

'See you next time I'm in town.' Penny smiled and stepped in, arms open for a hug.

'I'll call you tonight. See if you've uncovered any answers from our evidence yet.' Jenny grinned mischievously.

'That's what caller ID is for.' They laughed. 'Nah, I'll take your call. Talk tonight.' They hugged again, holding the embrace for a few seconds longer than before. Jenny pulled herself away reluctantly.

'Let's go Philips.' The Constable was already waiting at the door, keys jostling in his hand.

'Ready when you are Williams.'

Chapter 18

The wind howled, but no rust-coloured dust blew across the field today. The police Landcruiser swayed along the muddy track leading to one of the largest iron-ore mines in South Australia.

'The mining companies employ a lot of people out this way. They keep Coober Pedy alive in the middle of summer when the temperatures hit fifty in the shade and the tourists stop coming.' Philips explained, glancing at Jenny every so often, but returning his gaze quickly to the road ahead.

'So what you're saying is, *don't rock the boat* then?'

'Rock the boat but don't sink it.' Philips smiled. 'I know not rocking it isn't a thing for you.'

'Am I that obvious?' Jenny feigned hurt feelings, her hand over her heart, eyelashes fluttering. Philips' laughed aloud.

'You're just zealous and that's something we don't see out in the desert often Williams. Things move at a slower pace out here.'

Her Sergeant seemed to like it that way, but O'Connell was different. She found his calm temperament settling, like her dad. That is unless she talked about hunting down her aunt and cousin. She wasn't sure why he was against her taking the job in Coober Pedy. One day she might work up the courage to ask him.

'What's O'Connell's story?'

The Landcruiser hit a ditch at speed. Jenny's head nearly hit the roof. Philips grinned sheepishly.

'What do you mean?'

'Why's he still in town? He's almost the same age as Sarge. He could command his own station if he wanted to.'

Philips shrugged, then glanced over at Jenny. 'Keep your eyes on the road. I don't want another lift off.'

Philips focussed back on the road. 'He must just like it here.' Philips seemed to find the answer as unsatisfactory as she did. Jenny ran out of time to push the point as the entrance gates to the mine came into view.

'Does the HF pick up out here?' She asked as the vehicle turned right into the main driveway. Two ten-foot-high chain gates, complete with barbed wire and a large red 'STOP' sign plastered in the middle, halted their advance.

'Yeah. The mining companies have a huge tower that boosts the signal for their workers to keep in contact on UHF. The Police radio piggy-backs off it.'

'That's good. At least mining companies are good for something.'

'Why?' Philips eyebrows rose, then dipped into a frown.

'I don't know. I'm not a big fan of large-scale mining. I know we need it, but the corporations than run mining are powerful and ruthless at times.'

'They aren't above the law.'

'So why not just open the gate and let the Police Landcruiser right through?' Jenny lifted an eyebrow as Philips pressed the electric window button with another frown.

'Constables Philips and Williams. We need to speak with whoever's in charge of your vehicle allocation.'

The security guard on duty studied a clipboard in his hand. 'You're not on my running sheet for the day.'

Philips was taken aback a moment, but recovered quickly. 'Nope. This is an unscheduled call.'

'I'll need to radio for permission.' Jenny scoffed quietly, unnoticed by the guard but Philips pursed his lips at her.

They watched as the security guard returned to the gate office and spoke over the UHF radio. A moment later he returned to the vehicle, his clipboard forgotten.

'You been here before?' Philips shook his head. 'Go through the gate, turn left and head directly to the site office. These trucks will roll over you like tinfoil if you get in their way, so stick to the marked road and don't drive on past the office.'

'Gotcha.' Philips nodded vigorously.

The gates opened electronically. Philips drove through carefully, his eyes darting in all directions. Jenny gripped her seat by the fingernails as they passed two yellow trucks the size of small ships.

Philips turned left as instructed, pulling the Police vehicle up into one of three marked parking bays outside a transportable office. The white metal building was positioned on concrete pillars, in front of a gigantic shed. A row of roller doors that resembled vast caverns loomed, awaiting the massive trucks.

The ground rumbled as yellow strobing lights flashed out of the darkness. Philips gawked out the windscreen as a dinged-up pineapple coloured beast rolled by, the tiny driver perched in the air-conditioned cab like a mountaineer.

They undid their seatbelts, got out, checked their surroundings again, then slammed the doors of the four-wheel drive in unison.

'I'll explain what we found, if you don't mind.' Jenny suggested and Philips shrugged he didn't care one way or the other.

She secured her weapon by checking the belt clip was in place before leading the way up the dozen or so steps from the vehicle to the aluminium ramp leading to the office. She opened the glass panel door to a wave of cool air and a bottle-blonde receptionist with perfectly styled hair behind the counter. Her make-up was impeccable, her uniform ironed within an inch of its life. Her practised receptionist smile appeared with precision, stuck in place like a clown at the town fair.

'Officers. What can I help you with?'

'I'm Constable Williams, this is Constable Philips.' Jenny hoicked her thumb at Philips, the woman nodded but her face remained impassive. 'We'd like to speak with a couple of your workers please. They were driving a four-wheel drive north of here off the Coober Pedy, William Creek Road yesterday morning.'

'Do you have a registration number of the vehicle?' The woman's sing-song tone reminded Jenny of elevator music. It was supposed to be pleasant. It wasn't.

'No. Sorry. We have the approximate time and the vehicle will be missing a hubcap.'

The receptionist chuckled sardonically. 'I wish I could help you but we have over a hundred four-wheel drive vehicles in the fleet and I suspect more than one is missing a hubcap at this very moment.'

'Perhaps you have a logbook of vehicles that were off site yesterday morning? Maybe we could cross reference those with missing hubcaps?'

'We do, but I need either a warrant to make them available or my boss' permission.' The receptionist's jaw tightened. Jenny couldn't tell if it was fear of getting in trouble with her superior or a deliberate attempt to fob her off.

'Can you ask your boss then?'

'I'm afraid he's off site.'

Of course he is. 'Is there any chance you can just have a peek yourself and maybe tell me who was out there? This is extremely important.'

'I'm sorry. I can't do that. What's this about?'

Maybe she didn't know about Beth's body being found out there. If she did, she was doing an excellent job of hiding it, but that's what staff in mining offices were trained for. *Oh, we've hit a gas seam and its contaminating the local water course. Hush! Hush! Don't tell anyone. Maybe they won't notice.*

She knew she was generalising and if she spoke aloud, someone would likely consider her a conspiracy nutter. She was also fully aware that many families relied on the mining companies and most probably did the right thing, but still, there was something this woman wasn't saying.

'Our accident scene was taped off. It appears someone from your mining operation might have accidentally driven into the area. We just need to eliminate the vehicle from our investigation.'

Philips wandered around behind her. To anyone but her, he appeared bored, but Jenny saw him reach into his pocket to retrieve his mobile. He thumbed through the screen as though he were bored and killing time, but she knew he never used his mobile on duty.

'I can see how knowing the vehicle would help, but I can't see how I can assist you Officer Williams.' *At least she remembered her name!*

'I understand. I'll make a call and see if we can get a warrant to get the records sent over.'

The woman smiled without warmth as Jenny turned to see Philips gazing out the site office window.

'We done?' He asked too eagerly, confirming her suspicions.

She glanced back over her shoulder as the receptionist returned her eyes to the computer screen at her desk. She peered up one last time as Jenny approached the door.

'For now.' She couldn't help but make it clear she wasn't finished yet.

Philips opened the door. Jenny scuttled through. He followed close behind.

'What did you get?' she asked as they returned to their vehicle.

He smiled. 'I thought I was being stealthy.'

'You were. I don't think she noticed, but I've never seen you use that on the job.' She nodded toward the phone that was now back in his right-hand pants pocket.

'You know the old saying—returning to the scene of the crime?' Jenny smiled and nodded. 'Well there were two bozos lurking outside, studying our car like they should have had better things to do so I snapped a shot, just in case.'

'Well done Philips. I'm impressed.' He grinned sheepishly over the top of the car as they opened the doors and got back in.

Chapter 19

Jenny tapped out her report on the front office computer as Philips forced a sausage roll down his throat at breakneck speed.

She was so busy with no time to go over Nick's dad's suicide report or track down any new leads in her own missing family case. Solving her family mystery was still high on her priority list, but a girl was dead and although it wasn't murder, it was suspicious and needed her full attention.

She was abundantly aware of her promise to follow up on Nick's dad's case. She kept telling herself that helping Nick was helping her, but thinking of the cloud hanging over the suicide case made her wonder how many more cases former Senior Constable Len Holmes dropped the ball on.

He was now in prison, awaiting trial for the part he played in covering up Tiffany Cox's murder – her first case in her first week of arrival. She wished she could question him about her current case. Did he miss something back when Beth went missing? The only problem being he was held in Adelaide, far, far from her reach.

She pushed the thought aside. Instead, she filed her report into the case file which still bore only a number, no name—no formal identification made. The idea of another young woman going missing in Coober Pedy made her stomach knot. *Was Melanie tied up with a dog collar in someone's tin shed?*

There would be no peace for her until she uncovered what happened to her cousin and aunt. As much as she wanted a normal life, she wasn't going to get one. She'd dedicated years, training to be a cop for just this opportunity. A transfer to Coober Pedy was all she wanted since graduating high school.

'Hey, check this out!' Philips' voice snapped her out of her funk.

'What?'

'Check out this photo. I knew there was something familiar about one of the guys.'

O'Connell peered up from the filing cabinet, his office desk being occupied by Philips. He joined Philips. Leaning over his shoulder, pointing to the screen. 'Is that the two lads hanging around your vehicle at the mine?'

'Yeah. This one is Tom Grundy. Not sure about the other.'

'That's Luke Mitchell if I'm not mistaken.'

Philips studied the photo a moment before opening and closing his mouth, his brow creased. 'It could be Luke. I've not seen him for years, but I used to go to school with Tom. He's got long hair now, which is why I didn't recognise him right away.'

'Run them for any offences.'

'They probably won't have anything major. Mining companies don't like to employ anyone with any serious criminal history,' Jenny offered as she stepped up alongside O'Connell to look at the zoomed-in image of two men around Philips' age.

The first wore a long beard, his hair tied back in a low ponytail beneath a white hardhat with reflective tape around the brow.

The other was shorter than the first, his hair cropped short under his hardhat.

'Can we bring them in for questioning? The receptionist at the mining company might not want to share who they are, but if we already know now, she can't exactly stop us questioning them, can she?' Jenny asked.

'I'll call the manager of the mine and see what we can organise.' O'Connell reached for the desk phone. 'I can't warrant you two driving out there again today to speak to two guys who just happened to be hanging around your car. They might have been smoking weed in the dunnies when you rocked up and your presence just made them nervous for all we know.'

'True, but the mines drug test randomly.' Philips glanced toward Jenny. She nodded, but couldn't help but wonder if O'Connell was right and these two were unrelated to their case.

'What else have we got then?' Jenny asked Philips as O'Connell's call connected and they stepped away so he could speak without their voices in the background.

'We need to wait to hear about Murphy's interview.'

'What do we know about Murphy? Any family? I heard he's divorced. Who's the woman that was out there when I visited? Anna was her name. She sounded German or maybe Scandinavian.'

Jenny kept Nick's opinion of Mr Murphy to herself but there was one thing she was sure of – Anna was nervous. Sure, it could have been the weed, but maybe she knew more about who was holding Beth out in the middle of nowhere on Murphy's property?

'I think I can answer that question.' Jenny was surprised to see Sergeant Mackenzie enter the office, two people followed close behind. 'But that can wait for now. This is Mr and Mrs Thompson.'

Jenny watched the newcomers carefully, wondering why they would come all the way out to Coober Pedy when their daughter's body was already back in Adelaide, undergoing an autopsy.

'Mr and Mrs Thompson.' Jenny lifted the counter-top and stepped out. 'Are you staying in town?'

'I've booked them into the Opal.' Sarge started to move into the main office. 'Williams, you get them settled in. I'll bring you up to speed when you're done.'

Jenny didn't ask questions. Sergeant Mackenzie distanced himself so rapidly, it was obvious he wanted to create space between the Thompsons and himself. Was it because he'd lost a daughter? Or was it just his usual grumpy persona?

The only time she ever heard him give anyone a compliment was after she distracted Len Holmes from shooting or abducting him when they figured out it was his wife who killed Tiffany Cox not Len.

'Yes Sir.' Jenny saluted formally. 'Should I drive them over in your car? The road's still too muddy to walk through.' He threw her the keys and carried on walking away.

'Mr and Mrs Thompson. Please, follow me.' Jenny's head was spinning. She hoped neither of them asked her questions because she didn't believe she knew the answers they were likely looking for.

'Here.' Jenny opened the rear door of her boss's Nissan Navara. 'You can hop in the back if you like.'

'I'll ride up front with you, if you don't mind.' Jenny wasn't an expert in deciphering different US accents, but Mr Thompson's Californian influence was significant.

'Of course.' A hundred clichés crossed her mind—like sorry for your loss, but they didn't have a confirmed ID on the body yet, or did they? 'It's only just over the road, but the ground is still a little muddy. Don't want to get your shoes caked in it.' She knew she was rambling, but these could be the parents of the dead girl and that was just a horrible thought she didn't want to dwell on right now.

They rode in silence. The few minutes passed painfully as neither Mr nor Mrs Thompson spoke to each other. Jenny pulled up outside the Reception area of the Motel, happy to see a friendly face peering curiously out the window.

She didn't need to open the door for Mrs Thompson. Mr Thompson beat her to it. Instead, she scurried to the rear of the four-wheel drive to retrieve their luggage. Expecting to find a small overnight case, she was surprised when the barn doors opened to reveal two large suitcases.

Mr Thompson came around to collect the larger bags, leaving only a cosmetic bag for Jenny to carry. The idea that anyone needed such a huge bag of make-up in the middle of nowhere like central South Australia seemed strange, but one close look at Mrs Thompson explained a lot.

The woman's hair was as blonde as straw and almost as dry. Her eye make-up was heavy, with at least three applications of mascara, liquid eyeliner and carefully applied three tone eye-shadow. The lips were full, likely Botox induced and the dark apricot colour shone with a healthy coat of lip gloss. Considering they only just came off a small regional aircraft that flew from Adelaide to Coober Pedy, the woman presented impeccably well.

'Marj, these are the guests Sarge booked in.' Jenny didn't give their names. No doubt the Motel owner would have a million questions about why they were in town. She knew about the dead girl and nothing ever got past Marj, but she was the consummate professional too.

When Jenny first came to Coober Pedy, she avoided Marj's prying questions about Tiffany's murder on numerous occasions. The woman could smell a mystery from a mile away and loved to know everything that was going on in town. What she didn't know, she made up.

'Of course. Lovely to see you again Suzanna.' Marj came around the counter and hugged the woman as though they were long lost friends. 'Trent.' Was all she said to Mr Thompson. The exchange surprised Jenny, but it shouldn't have.

The couple likely stayed with Marj when Beth first went missing. Marj's memory was like an elephant. How else would she keep her finger on town gossip?

The cold shoulder to Trent was unexpected. Marj had never been like that with anyone. She always wore a broad smile to go with her gaudy clothing and bright red hair.

'I'll show you to your room. It's all prepared.' She glanced over her shoulder as she exited the Reception area. 'You coming for dinner in the restaurant tonight?' She couldn't be sure, but something in Marj's face told her it was an expectation, not a simple question.

'I'll let you know.' Marj didn't have time to insist as Jenny scuttled out of reception. Returning to work and finding out what was going on was top of her mind right now. Dinner plans were going to have to wait.

Chapter 20

Jenny kicked the mud from the bottom of her boots before entering the station. The red clay was like Clag and every step seemed to make it multiply. A rough scuff on the coarse mat outside removed enough to make it safe to walk over the worn lino flooring inside the station, but as she glanced back, she was overjoyed she wasn't the cleaner.

'Sorry. I was as fast as I could be.' Jenny rushed in, lifted the counter-top and stepped around, hoping not to have missed any of the Sergeant's update.

'Sarge was just telling us what he's been up to in Adelaide.' O'Connell didn't offer any details.

'I called in on Len Holmes before I picked up the Thompsons from the morgue.' Jenny waited. Interrupting her boss was never a good idea. 'Len remembered this case and offered a few insights into the Thompsons we might not have gotten from the file.'

Jenny understood the connotation. Personal insights on a case were never added to the official report. But her trust in Len's judgement wasn't exactly up there with Mother Theresa. The guy covered up Tiffany's murder to keep his wife out of jail and they all knew how badly that ended.

'Apparently, the parents were at loggerheads throughout the investigation. Mr Thompson thought Beth ran away, whereas Mrs Thompson insisted she was kidnapped.'

'Is there anything in the file to explain the difference of opinion?' Jenny sat down on the corner of O'Connell's desk and shook her head at the coffee Philips offered her.

'He said they argued, a lot.'

'That's not uncommon in this type of case. It's got to be exceptionally stressful losing a kid.' Philips spoke, then regarded Sergeant Mackenzie, realising what he just said, then blushed.

'I'd normally agree.' Mackenzie seemed not to notice Philips' discomfort, or did an excellent job of covering it up. Having lost his daughter in a car accident and then losing his marriage through the grief, made him only too familiar with what the Thompsons were going through. 'But Len said something was off about them from the start.'

'And you're happy to take Len's professional opinion on this one?' Jenny didn't hold back her scepticism.

O'Connell scowled at her. She sighed. 'What do you want us to do?' O'Connell returned his focus to the Sergeant.

'Just keep an eye on them. It's weird they are here, not in Adelaide with their daughter's remains. Why come out here? Why not just take her home to the US for burial?'

'It's definitely Beth Thompson's body then? Do we have a DNA match?'

Mackenzie shook his head to Jenny's question. 'We don't need DNA now. The parents have identified the body via a birth mark and they brought dental records with them that are a match.'

'There was no birth mark in the report.' Jenny stepped toward O'Connell's desk, ready to bring up the initial report.

'It was a mole, under the hairline at the back of her neck. They didn't think to mention it before her death, because it wasn't visible.'

'How did your interview with Murphy go?' Jenny sat back down on the corner of the desk.

'I've known Kent for years. He said he had no idea the shed at the derelict yards was being used for anything. Those stock yards and the storage shed were unused for at least two years.'

'Okay, but that doesn't explain where Beth was being kept before, when the yards were in use.'

'No.' Sarge rubbed his chin. 'It doesn't.'

'Sir. Do you know much about his divorce? His family?'

'He has a son. Gavin. He'd be in his early twenties now. When Kent and his wife Elaine divorced, he moved away with his mum, to Alice Springs, but I believe he's back on the property now.'

'I didn't see him out there when I visited with Nick Johnston.'

The Sergeant drew a long slow breath. 'Gavin was never very bright. He has a learning disability as far as I know, but he decided one school holidays that he wasn't going back to live with his mum. I think he liked the simple life, working on the station, riding bikes, doing his schooling by distance.'

'I'll see what I can find out about Murphy's workers.' Philips put his coffee down and moved to the front counter computer. 'And that Anna woman.'

'I told you I knew who she was.' The Sergeant sounded annoyed, enough to stop Philips in his tracks. 'She was a backpacker. Murphy needed someone to help with Gavin when he decided to stay. The two hit it off and Anna stayed on. Now she does the books, cooks, cleans.'

'Is she legal?' Jenny was surprised O'Connell asked the question that was running through her head.

'I hope so.' The Sergeant turned to toward his office, but stopped as he reached the door, turning back to Jenny, a serious look crossed his face. 'Watch the Thompsons and let me know if you find anything about any of Kent's workers before you do anything about it.' He glared hard into Jenny's eyes. 'You understand Williams?'

'Yes Sir. Nothing without your say-so Sir.' Sergeant Mackenzie studied her a moment, then turned and closed his office door.

'You dig into the workers Philips.' O'Connell pointed to the counter computer. Philips continued with what he started. 'Including Anna. Make sure her visa is up to date. Williams, you run as much background on the Thompsons as you can.' He rose from his desk. 'Use this computer. I'm going to grab some lunch.'

'Will do Sir.' Jenny traded places with the Senior Constable. Rolling his chair closer to the screen she ran a search on the internet for Beth Thompson, her mother Suzanna and her father Trent, including their last known address in Orange County USA.

She selected images first, wanting to be sure she found the right Thompsons. A page of photos of a stunning little girl with a broad smile, dark blonde ringlets and way too much makeup slowly populated her screen.

Jenny recognised the little girl immediately. The photo given to the police of Beth Thompson was nothing like these, but the little girl was undoubtedly the same Beth Thompson lying in autopsy in Adelaide.

Because of the way she was dressed, the makeup and the hairstyling, the girl presented five or six years older than her real age, making the resemblance to the seventeen-year-old girl she discovered broken and bleeding on the side of that muddy road, more easily recognisable.

Jenny continued her search, discovering more details on Mrs Thompson, and very little on her husband. It seemed Mr Thompson was a stock broker, but there were very few photos of him on the internet except a handful of professional profile shots. In contrast, Mrs Thompson appeared alongside her daughter at various pageants all over the west coast of the US.

It was an unnerving pile of photos showing mother and daughter with nearly as much makeup. In one photo, Beth was wearing a strapless dress that belonged on a senior high school prom queen, not a pre-pubescent child.

'Hey Philips. Check this out.' Jenny waved Philips over. He stepped behind her and studied the screen as she saved files and updated the case notes.

'Pageant Queen. She doesn't look eleven.'

'No. She's only ten in this photo.' Jenny tapped the screen.

'Old before her time.'

'Dead before her time.' Jenny added as Philips returned to the front counter. 'Anything on the workers at Murphy's?'

'I ran his son. Squeaky clean. I'll need to get a list of all the workers from Murphy's property to be sure, but that Anna, she's here on a resident working visa. Seems Kent Murphy sponsored her to stay.'

'Okay. I'll check in with Penny and see if the autopsy or tests have shown anything new to go on. I feel like we're getting nowhere on this.'

'Yeah. It appeared all cut and dried when the truck driver confessed but now it's so much more complicated. You really do know how to draw in the nasty ones Williams.'

Jenny didn't grace Philips with a response. They had been over this more than enough times now for her to know he was just messing with her. The grin on his face today confirmed it.

She picked up the desk phone and dialled the forensic lab in Adelaide. It was answered after a few rings.

'Forensics. Penny speaking.'

'Just the girl I needed to talk to.'

'I was just about to ring you.'

'You and I must be in sync. That happens a lot.' Penny laughed. 'What you got?'

'Nothing good I'm afraid. Well, helpful to the investigation maybe, but good, no.' Jenny waited. 'Did you know we confirmed ID?'

'Yes, Sarge said so. He brought the Thompsons back from Adelaide with him.'

'Really?'

'Yes, really. Strange hey.'

'For sure. I didn't meet them while they were here. It was Doc Holbrook who did the viewing with them, but why Coober Pedy?'

'Why indeed. What have you found that might help us work out where this poor girl has been for six years?'

'I've run the blood on the mattress. It's mostly foetal and placental. Nothing you wouldn't expect from a difficult birth.'

'So the blood all over her clothing at the scene was from the accident?'

'Yes and no. A lot of the blood you saw, and photographed was from her continual bleeding after giving birth. She didn't bleed much on scene because she almost certainly died instantly.'

Jenny sighed. 'What about the dirt under her nails?'

'Other than just that, dirt, there were traces of foetal blood, baby blanket fibres, hair, all accounted for.'

'Any idea why there was so much blood? Not that I'm an expert in giving birth, but has Doc calculated how much blood was left in the body versus how much was lost before the truck hit her?'

'She appears to have been haemorrhaging. She died on impact, her heart would have stopped pumping, but there could still be a small amount of seepage. Her post-mortem blood level indicates she lost close to forty percent of what someone her size and weight would usually have. That's low enough. Doc was surprised she hadn't already slipped into a coma. He is certain she was weak and disoriented when the truck hit her.'

'You think she might have ran out in front of the truck in a daze?'

'More like stumbled out is my guess. Also, you should know, the collar was covered in dog hair.'

'No human skin?'

'None, but there's something that Doc's just sent me that will raise the hairs on the back of your neck for sure.'

'What?' Jenny wanted to scream for Penny to spit it out. Her vision was already occupied with a re-enactment of Beth's last moments. The scene was horrific.

'The girl has no less than fifteen poorly healed fractures.' Jenny sucked in a quick breath and Philips turned to see why.

''Just when I thought the poor girl's life couldn't have been any worse. So none were set properly?'

'None.' They were each lost in thought a moment.

'Oh Penny. The poor kid. Whoever took her, beat her...'

'And didn't get her medical treatment.'

'They had to keep her a secret. It makes sense.'

'The Doc is going to have to date the injuries, but in the meantime, I'll add our findings to the case file. I'm still running tests on the foetal remains. I'll put a rush on the DNA so we can maybe find the father.'

'That will be a huge help. Thanks Penny.'

'Wait up, not so quick. How's Nick doing?' Jenny could hear the smile in her friend's voice.

'What do you mean?' Jenny tried to sound casual. Thinking about Nick made her cheeks flush. Philips was still looking at her, waiting for an update from the test results. 'I've got to run, but I'll call you this weekend. I'm heading out there to run down a few leads.'

She kept the conversation vague, hoping Penny would understand she couldn't talk now and Philips would think she was still talking about the case.

'You better and Jenny, don't make everything about the past. You know you have to let your hair down at some point.'

'Karaoke with you and Nev was as loose as I'm getting so get used to it.'

Penny laughed. 'Bye.'

'Bye.' Jenny hung up and turned her attention to Philips, ready to get on with a quick debrief, but the smile on his face said mentioning the karaoke episode on her first day was probably not a good idea.

'I still have the photos you know.'

'Destroy them.' Jenny warned with a shake of her finger.

'Now where would the fun be in that?'

Philips chuckled and Jenny sighed. She certainly made a strong impression on the locals with that first night at the Motel restaurant. She drank too much beer to remember how or why Nev and Penny convinced her to join them on stage, but even she smiled at the memory. What she recalled of it anyway.

'It seems Beth Thompson sustained multiple fractures, all having healed badly, likely with no medical intervention.' Jenny decided to change the subject to something safer.

'So our kidnapper is a nasty piece of work.'

'We have to find him Philips. He's lost his toy and that could mean he'll be looking for a new one.'

Chapter 21

Jenny threw Nev's keys on the round timber kitchen table, dumped her backpack on a chair and stumbled to her bedroom. She stopped outside the bathroom on the way. The door was closed, which was code for someone was in there, since it didn't have a lock.

The boys would have gotten back from their early shift a few hours ago and as much as Jenny wanted a shower, she wasn't in the mood to hang out in the kitchen and wait for whoever was inside to finish.

She pushed her door closed, before flopping down on her bed, a sigh escaping her lips involuntarily. The photos of her cousin and aunt that she kept in the dressing table mirror frame at the Motel now sat on the rickety bedside table to her right.

Rolling over on her side, she reached for the photo of Melanie. The petite dark blond was smiling, as she always seemed to be, but Jenny noticed a sadness in her eyes that she must have missed before. What was on Melanie's mind that Spring? Why did Aunt Carolyn take them away to the bush for a holiday?

The more she considered the idea that two women would trundle off to Coober Pedy and William Creek Station the more she wondered over it. Sure, taking Melanie away for a break before university made sense, but the Gold Coast in sunny Queensland seemed like a more sensible place.

A thud on the door made her jump. 'Jenny. We are heading to town for dinner. You coming?' Tim's voice sounded hollow through the thick timber.

'I'm pretty knackered Tim. I think I'll give it a miss.'

'Come on. It's not the same without you there.' His voiced sounded teasing and she was sure he was visualising her and Nev screaming out *ABBA's Dancing Queen*, but it wasn't Karaoke night.

A small voice in her head begged her to get off the bed and go an enjoy life more. She was here for a purpose, but it was becoming all-encompassing—holding her back from enjoying her new friends. Everyone kept telling her life was too short and her job, with cases like Tiffany and Beth only proved it.

'Okay.' She sounded lame even to her own ears. 'Is the shower free? I need to freshen up.' She opened her door to find Tim standing with a towel around his waist, his wet ginger, almost strawberry blonde hair dripping down his chest.

She smiled, thinking about what Penny would say right now, but averted her eyes.

'Get some bloody clothes on man.' Nev slapped Tim gently on the bare shoulder. 'The shower is all yours.'

'Thanks. I'll only be ten minutes.'

'Take your time.' Nev offered as he pulled a tight-fitting T-shirt over his head, covering his sculptured abs.

Jenny grabbed her towel and headed for the bathroom, her mind filled with half-naked men. She reminded herself that there was a significant difference between letting her hair down and sleeping with one of her house mates. Nick's piercing blue eyes came to mind. Was that relationship going anywhere? Did she even want it to?

She scolded herself for being juvenile and Nick's eyes were quickly replaced by the unanswered question in Melanie's. Ten minutes, she reminded herself as she turned the hot water on.

****

The smell of beer, sweat and steak made Jenny's stomach grumble as they entered the Motel restaurant. *So much for home cooked meals,* Jenny thought as the three of them found seats at a long table in the middle of the dining area.

'I'm buying the beers this time.' Jenny rushed toward the bar. Nev's habit of not letting her buy anything was getting old. Besides, she didn't need to be owing anyone any favours. When they first met, it was clear there was an attraction, but Jenny quickly put him straight.

Cheryl hovered behind the bar, her face still showing the pain of losing her closest friend. 'Hey Cheryl. Can I grab a jug of beer thanks?'

'Sure.' The woman sounded flat.

'What time do you get off?' Jenny watched Cheryl expertly pour the jug and place it on the towelling runner that went the full length of the highly polished timber bar.

'It's not so busy tonight, so I think after the dinner rush. Nine maybe.'

'Why don't you join us for a beer?' Jenny hoicked her thumb toward the table where Nev and Tim sat, heads together, no doubt chatting about work. Nev and Tim saw a lot of each other around the hospital most days and seemed to get along well.

'I don't know. I don't want to cramp your style.' Jenny frowned, then remembered Cheryl and Nev shared some history.

'You won't. I'm not dating either of them. In fact. I'm not dating at all.'

Cheryl's eyebrow rose. 'Why not?'

'It's a long story. Join me for a beer and I'll fill you in.'

Cheryl's face lit up in a rare smile. Jenny spotted a dimple on her right cheek as she pulled three chilled glasses from the fridge below the bar. 'Thanks. I'd like that.'

'Great. Talk soon.' She waved her credit card over the machine and didn't wait for a receipt.

Weaving between the sparsely occupied tables, with three glasses stacked high in one hand, the jug in the other, she failed to notice the Motel door open.

When she gazed up, she stopped, her mouth hung open a moment before she forced it closed.

In the doorway, stood Nick Johnston, complete with moleskin trousers, riding boots and his ever-present Akubra hat. She couldn't help but wonder what he was doing in town, but focussed on getting beer to her friends instead of staring at Nick.

'Nice.' Nev rose and helped her place the jug on the table. She was sure it wasn't chivalry, but a rising thirst for a pint of beer that drove him.

'Cheryl is going to drop in for a beer when she finishes her shift. I hope that's okay?'

'Sure,' both guys chimed in simultaneously.

'Let's order. I'm starved. Today was hectic.' Tim pushed the menu to Jenny, but she knew it by heart now. After a month living in the hotel, there wasn't anything on the menu she hadn't yet tried. Maybe Marj would update it soon? She hoped so.

'You guys order. I need to check with Marj about something.' She didn't wait for their responses, but as she hastened toward the exit, she saw Nick still standing nearby. He looked lost, but his eyes fixed on her like an anchor.

'Hey,' he muttered as she reached him.

'Hi. Do you come here often?' It was a stupid thing to say. She knew he didn't and it sounded like a pick-up line gone terribly wrong, but she grinned stupidly to make it seem like she intended it that way.

'No, but I should make the effort more often.'

'It's a long drive. Do you want to join us?' Nick studied the two men laughing and drinking the jug of beer way too rapidly.

'Friends of yours?'

Did she note a touch of jealousy in his tone?

'Roommates, yep.'

'Roommates?'

Yep, definitely a tone.

'They were both super friendly when I moved here and when I wanted to move out of the Motel , they offered their spare room.'

'I bet they did.'

Jenny ignored Nick's scepticism. 'Come on over. I know you know Nev from the hospital. Have you met Tim before?' She reached for his hand and was relieved he didn't resist as she pulled him toward the table.

'I need to see Marj, but I'll be back in a second. Cheryl's joining us later. I know it's not a weekend or anything, but it would be nice to have a little catch up with a few locals.'

She knew she was waffling on, but Nick was never much of a talker and the urge to speak into the silence was compelling.

'Nev, Tim. You know Nick, right?' Both men stood and shook his hand, muttering pleasantries. 'Can you pour him a beer in my unused glass? I'll grab another when I get back from catching Marj.'

She left them there hoping they could find something in common to chat about while she chased down Marj's spare vehicle for the weekend. She passed Mr and Mrs Thompson on the covered veranda, heading toward the restaurant.

They nodded to her, both looking solemn but she couldn't expect anything else. They now knew their missing daughter was dead and they were here for answers. Jenny was familiar with the need to know the circumstances of someone going missing, but she was uneasy about their visit to Coober Pedy.

'Marj.' She strolled into Reception and smiled at the red-headed Motel owner who always seemed to be on the front desk, a smile in place that was never forced.

'Jenny. Glad you could make it for dinner.'

'What's the occasion?'

'Oh, nothing too special. What can I do for you?'

'I'm planning on heading back out to William Creek Station on the weekend and wondered if I can borrow the old Navara?'

'Oh. Honey! I'm so sorry but I've leant it to Suzanna and her husband.' Jenny wondered over the lack of personal pleasantries with Mr Thompson but was too focussed on why they wanted a car.

'Oh. Bummer. That's fine. Do you know why they need the car?' The investigator in her was pushing forward.

'None of my business luv.' That was so unlike Marj who kept abreast of even the smallest bit of gossip in town.

'What's your history with Mr and Mrs Thompson anyway?'

'They stayed here during the initial investigation into Beth's disappearance. That's why I recognised Beth's necklace, I just couldn't place it.'

'That makes sense. You seem very familiar with Suzanna, but you don't appear to like Trent very much?'

'Oh that. It's nothing.' Jenny could see it was far from nothing. Something worth investigating. Marj's nose was ultra-sensitive. If she didn't like Trent Thompson, then maybe there was something worth fishing for.

'I've got to get back to the dining room before Nev and Tim chew off their own arms.' Jenny turned to leave.

'I'm sorry about the car luv.'

'It's fine Marj. I'll work something out.' As she made her way back to the restaurant, the sound of an agitated voice caught her attention. She couldn't make out the words, but the voice was male, hushed and annoyed.

The cop in her couldn't ignore the sensation the tone in the man's voice invoked. Following the voice, she ducked her head around the corner of the building near the restaurant entrance, to find Suzanna and Trent Thompson in a heated discussion.

To stay undetected, she pulled back against the side glass of the main entrance, straining to listen. The conversation stopped abruptly. Suzanna appeared around the corner, her expression unreadable. Jenny turned to open the glass door, trying to look as casual as possible but certain she failed miserably.

The hairs on her neck stood on end as she sensed Suzanna's eyes on her back. Questions raced through her mind as she digested the scene. It was too confusing to make sense of. Nick rose slightly as she returned to the table, dragging her mind back to the three men sitting together at the long table.

'You took a while?' Nick's blue eyes searched her face.

'Sorry. I was trying to borrow Marj's spare four-wheel drive but she's loaned it to someone.'

'What did you need it for?' Nick pushed a beer toward her as she sat. 'I grabbed another glass for you.'

'Thanks.' She steadied her nerves with a long sip. What was it about the scene between the Thompsons that rattled her? 'I wanted to head back out to your place this weekend and Nev has an Uncle out that way I need to catch up with, about that case I've been working on.'

Nick studied her a moment, then realised what case she was referring to. 'I can come and get you.'

'No, it's too far. You've already come in tonight.'

'I can take you.' Nev offered. 'I'm off this Saturday afternoon.'

'It's okay mate. I'll be back in town again for more supplies.' Did Nick stiffen slightly, or was it Jenny's imagination?

Nev sipped his beer, his eyes on Nick's. 'I need to introduce her to my uncle anyway. She can't just rock up at the Community without an invite.'

Nick took a swig of beer, stared a moment, then nodded without a reply. But a slight huff said he wasn't happy.

'Thanks Nev.' Jenny attempted to break the stare-off between the two men. Nev knew where he stood with her, so why was he goading Nick?

'So what's the big occasion?' Everyone turned to Tim and Jenny was thankful he broke the tension.

'What occasion?' Jenny knew she was missing something important, but couldn't put her finger on it.

'Nick's in town. Marj is being secretive.' Tim scanned around conspiratorially. 'There has to be something special going on,' he grinned.

Nick and Nev shrugged in unison, causing Jenny to smile on the inside. One, the landholder of William Creek Station, the other related to the local indigenous custodians. The idea that they were sitting together in the local Motel bar seemed right somehow.

Chapter 22

Cheryl collected the dishes from the table. 'I'll join you guys in a few minutes, if that's still okay?'

'Of course.' Jenny jumped up. 'Can I help you with those?'

'Don't be silly. You're a local police officer and a paying customer. Marj would have my guts for garters if I let you help.' Cheryl seemed more relaxed, a smile stirring at the corners of her mouth made her look prettier.

'Okay, if you're sure. See you in a sec then.'

Nick rose. 'I better be heading off. I've got a long drive home tonight.'

'You can crash on the couch at our place if you want.' Nev offered. 'Or maybe you have other plans.' He winked and lifted his near empty schooner toward Jenny. She wanted to kick him under the table but he was too far away.

'I have a ton of work to get done tomorrow.' He glanced at his watch as though he were still tossing up the idea of staying in town.

Nev jumped up and headed for the bar, empty jug in hand. 'Decision made. I'll get the next round.'

Nick sat back down and whispered in Jenny's ear, 'These guys can drink,' the warmth of his breath tickled her neck, causing her stomach to flutter like a schoolgirl.

'Med students. They are a special breed.' She returned the whisper, her lips only a few inches from Nick's made them both stop. Tim coughed as Nev dropped the jug of beer on the table with a heavy hand.

No one spoke, but they didn't have any time to consider the mood as Cheryl slid into a chair alongside Nev and the lights dimmed throughout the large restaurant. A spotlight hit the tiny stage at the rear, near where the breakfast buffet usually set up.

The restaurant was nowhere near capacity, but Jenny spotted a few regulars, including Sergeant Mackenzie, Philips and his wife, and Senior Constable O'Connell, all sitting at a table by the stage.

'Did Marj ever tell you the story about how she came to buy the Motel?' Nev called across the table as a hush settled on the room. Jenny shook her head. 'I think you're about to find out.' He whispered loud enough for her to hear past Nick whom she noted strategically placed himself between them.

'Ladies and gentlemen. For one night only, the magnificent, the fabulous, the utterly vivacious, Liza Minelli, Coober Pedy style.' Stan the barman occupied the spotlight, a beer in hand, his mouth pressed up against the mic stand.

'It's her birthday and she'll party if she wants to. Take it away Marj!' The spotlight flashed from the barman to the side of the stage where a full-busted woman posed in stiletto heels, top hat and not much else.

Her mic was raised at an angle, her head tilted back, her right hand holding the rim of the hat. As the first words left Marj's lips and reverberated around the room, the crowd exploded with cheers and wolf whistles.

Jenny was sure this was not the first time Marj had jumped on that little stage, but it was her first appearance since the new constable moved to town. From miner to Motel owner, Marj was full of surprises. Her voice was gutsy, hitting every note perfectly.

The older woman owned the stage, prancing around in her six-inch heels like she wore them every day of her life. Her tight black leotard was topped with a sequined waist coat that hugged her figure, forcing her ample bosom high up and almost out over the top.

Everyone joined in on the chorus of *Big Spender.* Even Nick seemed to be toe-tapping and singing along with the show.

Three songs later, Marj tossed her top hat into the audience, flourished a bow before making her exit from the stage. The lights came up quickly, the clapping and laughter hung around as the chanting for an encore began. Marj obliged with practised grace and an abundance of willingness.

When the stage finally cleared in earnest, Jenny turned to Nick, then Nev. 'Am I the only person in town who doesn't know this story?'

'Yep.' Nev offered as he downed the rest of his beer.

'Care to elaborate?'

'I told you it's Marj's story to tell.' He nodded to the woman herself as she approached their table, a grin from ear to ear, an excited energy in every step she took.

Jenny rose to greet her. 'Why didn't you say it was your birthday?'

'Because I just love surprises.' Her grin widened, her eyes twinkled and Jenny wondered where the woman found such exuberance. 'Surprise!'

Everyone laughed as Marj pulled out a chair and collapsed into it with dramatic exaggeration.

'Care to tell me *that* story everyone knows except me?' Jenny sat back down, lifting the jug to offer Marj a beer. She shook her head gently.

'I've got my birthday cocktail coming. Stan knows the drill.' She glanced over her shoulder as though she were expecting him any second.

'This is an annual event then?' Jenny scanned the faces around the table, one eyebrow lifted.

'Of course.'

'So you all knew, all along?' She caught everyone's eye one at a time, landing on Nick last. He shrugged.

'Hey, I don't come into town too often. This is a first for me.' Nick's eyes were smiling, something that made Jenny's skin tingle and her stomach tumble. 'I got a special invite. No idea I've been missing such a great show all these years. I nearly left early too.'

'Well you went off to University and forgot all about a lot of stuff Mr Johnston.' Marj waggled her finger.

'The story!' Jenny insisted, Marj laughed, placed her hand on Jenny's before taking a big breath to indicate it was going to be a long one.

And it was.

Ten minutes later, long after Marj's cocktail arrived, she was winding up the tale. Jenny held her side and struggled to breathe between laughs as Marj carried on undeterred, her face alight with energy, her hands waving in the air telling the elaborate story, word by rehearsed word.

'There I was, drunk, not dressed like this, still covered in a day of dust and crap from mining. I belted out, a bit like you did that first night, song after song from Shirley Bassey, Liza, Barbara Streisand. You know it, I sung it.' Marj stopped to take a sip of her cocktail, the straw avoiding her mouth at all costs until she grabbed it and held it still.

'Anyway. Cut a long story short.' She snorted at the irony. 'I shacked up with the owner of this fine establishment and when he died, Jason left me the Motel.' Another sip of her cocktail found ice.

She stared at the bottom of the drink as it seemed to signify the end of what sounded like a fine, very unexpected love affair. 'He was the love of my life.' She swallowed hard, her eyes still searching the bottom of her glass. 'So, I stayed here, running this place.' She gazed up, swept her arm around

111

the room, her eyes finishing on Jenny's face. 'Everyday here reminds me of Jason.' She fell silent.

'You put on a great show Marj.' Tim patted her on the shoulder, dragging her from her sudden melancholy. The vivacious smile the woman usually wore returned with gusto.

'So when I saw you singing with Nev and that forensic scientist, Penny, I thought here's a girl who can follow on in my tradition.

Jenny put up her hand. 'No way Marj. You know how much I hate being front and centre.'

'What did I miss?' Nick looked confused, his eyes searching Jenny's, then Marj's face.

'This one here, once you get enough beer into her, can belt out a song or two. She'll rock your socks off mate,' Nev offered and Jenny thought about how much she wanted to rock Nick's socks off and how it had nothing to do with belting out ABBA songs or Karaoke nights at the Motel.

Chapter 23

Jenny filed another lot of paperwork into the top drawer of the battered metal four-drawer cabinet, wondering why on earth anyone still used a paper trail. Sergeant Mackenzie was old-school in so many ways, the most obvious being his need to contain any case that might upset the locals.

O'Connell watched her slam the drawer closed, his eyes peering over reading glasses like a school professor. She noted he only recently started wearing spectacles. His thick salt and pepper hair made him look like a police officer from a day-time soap, but the glasses seemed to age him beyond his years.

'Those miners should be back in town by now Williams. Their shift ended this morning. You and Philips head to Tom's mum's place.'

'On it Sir.' Where Tom's mum's place was, was a mystery to Jenny but Philips seemed confident. 'Are we calling in a detective from Alice or Adelaide on this yet Sir?' O'Connell peered over at Sergeant Mackenzie's closed door and shook his head.

With a sigh, Jenny collected her service weapon from the safe, checked the safety was on and placed it in the waist holster before pulling on her utility vest.

'You better get to them quickly, before they hit the pub. The mine is alcohol free so most miners are usually straight into the closest pub or bar when their swing ends.' O'Connell adjusted his glasses like he was trying to decide exactly where on his nose they were most comfortable.

'Will do Sir,' Philips answered as he collected the keys to the police Landcruiser and headed out the door without confirming Jenny was following behind.

'Have the Thompsons asked for a detective yet Sir?' O'Connell glanced sideways as Sergeant Mackenzie appeared at his office doorway.

'Williams. You really need to learn to follow protocol.' She never intended for him to overhear the conversation, but since he did, maybe he should consider her question.

'Sarge. If that was your daughter, found like that, wouldn't you want a detective on the case? Wouldn't you be screaming for the most experienced person to find out exactly what happened to your daughter?'

Jenny resisted the urge to put her hands on her hips. She didn't want to antagonise her sergeant, not when he seemed to realise where she was going with the question.

'I see what you mean.' He scanned O'Connell's face, then his eyes rested on her once more. 'Have you run a background check on the Thompsons?'

'I didn't run police records, they are US citizens, but I've done a little digging'

'Anything the family might not want us to know?'

'Beth was a pageant princess, Suzanna a typical pageant queen mum. Father's a stock broker.' Jenny ran through what she discovered yesterday, which wasn't much.

'O'Connell, get on and see if you can dig up any international police files.'

He turned from O'Connell's desk and instead of heading back to his office, he strolled toward the door. 'I'll be busy the rest of the afternoon. Keep me posted with anything new.'

As Sergeant Mackenzie left the station, Jenny turned to Senior Constable O'Connell who seemed to be left holding the honour of Boss again for the afternoon. As though he could read her thoughts, O'Connell lifted a hand and shook his head, telling her not to ask the question that was on her mind.

'Have you gotten anywhere with your cold case?' She grinned at his tactful change of subject.

'I'm heading out to see Nev's uncle this weekend. Like I mentioned to you the other day, he told Nev the William Creek Station was cursed in some way. I'd like to know if this supposed curse has anything to do with my cousin, maybe even Nick's dad's death.'

'That's a long stretch. Don't you think?'

Jenny never mentioned her question over Nick's dad's death before. Not to O'Connell. It just slipped out, and she expected a question. *Why hadn't he even blinked at the idea?*

Did he have his own suspicions about the suicide report? Jenny opened her mouth to speak, but Philips appeared at the front door.

'When you're ready!'

'Sorry Philips.' Jenny's studied O'Connell a moment before she spun around and jogged to the exit, her mind racing with more questions than answers.

****

Tom's mum confirmed they were indeed too late to catch the boys before they made the most of their first day of alcohol freedom.

A search of the local hot spots led them to the Opal Inn Underground Bar. Jenny followed Philips down the wide hand-cut sandstone steps to a dimly lit cavern that she strained to see the back of. A sea of high-vis shirts and Akubra hats in equal measure filled the space. They waded to the bar, carefully navigating the crowd that were well into their Friday lunchtime drinking session.

'I'm not sure these two will be in any state to help us out today.' She spoke from just behind Philips' shoulder. He glanced back, the look on his face saying he totally agreed with her.

115

She reached the bar as a tall, lean barman with long grey hair pulled back in a ponytail made fleeting eye contact, before returning to study the glass he was drying. His exposed biceps bore rough tattoos – the five-dot black ink on the back of his hand said he served prison time. He appeared unfazed by two uniformed police officers. Jenny wasn't sure if that was a good sign. She stepped up to the bar. He didn't look at her, even when she spoke.

'Looking for Luke Mitchell or Tom Grundy. Seen either of them this afternoon?'

The barman shrugged, his eyes still on the glass in his hands. Philips tapped her on the shoulder. She turned, he pointed down the bar to a group of fluorescent orange shirts sitting in a high-back booth.

The high-backed timber bench-seats rose up against the wall to merge into the sandstone walls. A dim light hung above the table, beer glasses filled almost every inch of the space, most empty, a few still partially full.

They stepped away from the bar, weaving their way through a growing crowd. Jenny avoided two beer spills, but the third landed on her boot, which was already red with dry, caked-on mud from days of traipsing around the countryside.

The Jackaroo responsible for the spill was ready to give her a mouthful, until he realised she was female. His expression changed, his smarmy grin sent a shiver down her spine. She raised her hand to ward off anything that was about to leave his mouth, but he spoke anyway.

'If I'd known the coppers would be so pretty I'd have joined the force.'

She smirked, hoping her sarcasm was conveyed, before pressing on toward her targets.

Neither Tom nor Luke noticed two fully armed officers in uniform working their way toward them. Not even as they drew up alongside one another, facing the group of five men, their thighs pressed against the table.

'Tom, Luke.' Philips broke the ice.

The thinner of the two men gazed up, his eyes glazed over enough for them to know he wasn't going to be any use for a few hours, maybe more. The second, shorter man recognised Philips, and seemed to focus on the fact they were both in uniform.

'Danny is that you?' He tried to focus by pulling back from the officer and squinting his eyes. 'How long has it been?'

'Tom. About five years. I didn't realise you were back in town.'

'Working at the Santrose Mine.'

'Really?'

Jenny was impressed. Philips was doing a fantastic job of looking surprised over the news.

'Yeah mate. Great money and a hell of a lark really.'

'About that.' Philips waited for his words to start to set in. 'I was out there the other day.' The conversation next to Tom stopped. Luke's bleary eyes focussed instantly, making Jenny wonder just how drunk he might be.

'I saw you and Luke hanging around my police Landcruiser.' Philips waited. His timing was perfect as Luke tried to push his way past the two other miners sitting next to him, neither was budging. Tom, somehow sensing there was no easy escape, sank down in his seat, slowly dropping below the edge of the table, out of sight.

Jenny grinned at Philips, trying desperately not to laugh. 'Was he planning on crawling out from underneath?' She spoke quietly to Philips, who stepped back and peered under the table, his face turned back to her, a grin spread slowly over his features before he chuckled and straightened.

117

They were genuinely wasted. Questioning them while under the influence was unethical and probably a useless waste of time, but a few hours in the cells at the station would likely sort them out.

'You take him.' Jenny pointed to Tom as his head poked out from under the table. Philips nodded as she hoicked a thumb at the two miners blocking Luke's exit. They slid out without a word. Jenny crooked her finger at Luke as Philips intercepted Tom, stumbling to his feet from under the table.

'We need to ask you a few questions mate. About the accident site out on the William Creek, Coober Pedy Road.' Philips didn't bother to handcuff Tom. It was enough of an effort to bring him to his feet from his hands and his knees that it was obvious he wasn't going to successfully abscond or be a threat.

'We'll give you two a few hours to sober up.' Jenny assured them as they led the stumbling pair up the stairs into the main street and out of the first decent dugout Jenny had seen in town so far.

'Don't say anything Luke.' Tom slurred his words as Luke shook his head. Jenny wasn't sure if he was agreeing to his friend's suggestion or not, but neither of them spoke as they were pushed into the back of the Landcruiser, Jenny alongside, Philips driving.

Chapter 24

Philips entered the interview room, pulling out the seat alongside Jenny. Tom sat across from them, sober now, his eyes fixed on his clasped hands resting on the table.

An earlier discussion over who to interview first led to Philips suggesting Tom was a good choice. He believed he could read the former classmate more easily than Luke.

Philips started the recording and asked Tom the usual questions for the record before commencing the interview.

'Tom.' The miner glanced up for the first time. 'We know you and Luke were out at the accident site on William Creek Road Tuesday, we just want to know what you were out there for.'

'We weren't out there.' His eyes dropped to his clasped hands again. He held his hands so tightly together that his knuckles were white from the lack of blood flow, his shoulders tense. Everything about his body language screamed that he was lying. But Jenny couldn't understand why.

'Look. We're willing to overlook the fact you tampered with a crime scene.' Philips carried on assuming Tom had been out on the scene. 'We just need to know if you saw anything useful.'

Tom's eyes flicked up to focus on Philips, the knuckles on his hands finally showing some sign of colour. He searched Philips' face, a mix of mistrust and familiarity at war in his eyes.

'I didn't see anything except the taped off area.' Familiarity might have won out.

Jenny glanced over at Philips who didn't return eye contact, he remained focussed on Tom. His interview technique was interesting to watch, considering that when Jenny first arrived in Coober Pedy, she was worried Philips' association with the locals might make it hard for him to be objective.

And she was right. He totally missed Len's involvement in Tiffany's murder. Maybe it had been a wakeup call —policing the town and keeping the people in it safe was what the job was all about.

'Alright. So why were you out there?' Philips continued with his fixed stare on Tom's face. The accusation in his eyes told Tom he knew there was more to the trip out than a joy ride.

'We heard about the accident. Just rubbernecking I guess.'

Jenny and Philips knew he was lying.

'Interesting.' Philips' tone was hard even for Jenny to read. *Damn he was getting good at this.*

'Look! Alright! A mate was roughing it out there with his girl and well, we heard about the dead girl and we wanted to check on our mate.'

Jenny resisted the urge to join the interview. Tom was talking. The last thing they needed was to break Philips' connection, but she found it difficult to remain quiet as her adrenalin kicked in. The idea Tom and Luke may know Beth's abductor set her senses on fire.

'What's your mate's name? And his girl?' Philips realised he should have stuck with one question at a time, but too late.

Tom's eyes went a little wild before he closed his mouth, his gaze darting back to his restrained hands.

Philips sighed, his apologetic gaze fell on Jenny, but she gave him a slight shake of her head to say it was okay.

'Did you find out if the victim of the accident was your friend's girl?' Jenny changed tack. Tom seemed to respond.

'We still don't know.'

'You've not seen your mate then?' Tom shook his head, but didn't make eye contact. 'If I showed you a photo of the girl would you know if it was her or not?'

Tom's eyes slowly rose to look closely at Jenny's expression. She plastered a sympathetic look on her features, complete with sad eyes to emphasize her empathy for his friend's possible loss. In honesty, it wasn't hard. Thinking of Beth made her sad without effort.

Finally, Tom nodded. Jenny took a deep breath, forcing herself to move slowly, without too much eagerness. She flipped open a folder, facing it towards her at first to ensure Tom couldn't read anything important from within. Calmly she drew out the morgue photo of Beth Thompson. Placing it on the table, she rotated it around slowly to face Tom and waited, trying to take carefully measured breaths.

'Is the baby okay?'

Jenny and Philips simultaneously drew a quick breath. Clearly neither of them was as composed as they thought they were.

'You know who this is then?' Jenny carried on taking the lead. Tom nodded. 'We are having difficulty identifying her.' She lied. 'Do you know her name?'

'Tash.' Jenny glanced over to Philips again. She told herself she needed to stop doing that. *Stay focussed.*

'Does Tash have a last name?' Tom shrugged. 'Can you speak for the recording please?'

'Not that I know.'

'You said she was living with her boyfriend. Do you know where they were staying?' Jenny kept Beth's true identify to herself.

Tom wasn't in a hurry to answer. His suspicion growing.

'The baby wasn't with Tash.' She knew exactly where the baby was, but Tom didn't know that.

Tom squirmed, his gaze growing restless, darting from her to Philips, then back at his hands. 'They moved around a lot. His old man would have freaked if he knew about Tash, and the baby.'

'Where were they most recently then?' Jenny desperately wanted to ask who the boyfriend was, but knew a direct question now would end the interview in a heartbeat. She wanted to know if Tom knew of any other location apart from the shed on Murphy's property. If he didn't, they might have been able to track down the boyfriend there.

'I don't know!' His eyes darted to Philips and back again, the pain in his gaze told her he legitimately cared. 'I'd tell you if I did, honest. She was due soon, but Ga…the dad was working away.'

'Okay.' Jenny spoke softly. 'Just relax and tell us what you do know. The baby was due soon. How do you know that?'

'The dad told us.'

'So you've met Tash before. You knew she was pregnant. Where did you meet her?'

Tom was wringing his hands now, the stress mounting. 'Out on Murphy's station.'

'In the old cattle yard shed? Anywhere else?' Jenny prodded. Tom shrugged, suddenly realising he said too much.

'Is Gavin the father Tom?' His eyes dropped to his hands. 'You're not in trouble… yet, but if you don't come clean Tom, we'll charge you with disturbing a crime scene for starters.' Jenny wanted to say kidnapping and statutory rape but she managed to keep her cool.

'He'll be wrecked when he finds out it was Tash in the accident.' Tom finally gave her the information she needed. It surprised her. Not the information, but that Tom honestly thought Gavin cared for Beth.

They were missing something. Something vitally important and the look on Philips' face told Jenny she wasn't alone in her thinking. Sarge's request to dig deeper into the Thompson family just topped her most important things to do list.

Chapter 25

Jenny peered inside Sergeant Mackenzie's office to find the high-backed seat empty once again. Turning, she saw O'Connell studying her.

'What's up?'

'Where's Sarge?'

'You heard him. He said he'd be out the rest of the day.' O'Connell's tone was matter of fact.

'We need to find Gavin Murphy.'

'Why do you need to speak to Gavin?' O'Connell put his pen down.

'He's Beth's baby's father and possibly her captor.'

O'Connell beckoned her to his desk with the wiggle of his finger. 'Start at the beginning Williams.'

'Okay. Tom and Luke, after separate interviews agree that Beth was willingly, or appeared to be willingly living with Gavin Murphy. Last seen in the old yard shed we found. They confirmed she was pregnant and Gavin was the father. Neither would give us any other locations he's been staying at. Either they don't know or won't tell.'

O'Connell frowned, then rubbed his chin and considered the information. 'Gavin is only a few years older than Beth Thompson.'

'Exactly Sir.'

'So he would have been what, fifteen when she went missing?'

'Philips and I shared the same thought. Either he's a sick little son of a bitch or he didn't abduct Beth at all.'

'So, if he didn't abduct her, but someone else did, maybe he helped her escape the kidnapper?'

'Or did she run away from her parents to begin with? Her dad thought so. Holmes told us as much.' Why did Mr Thompson believe she ran away? What from?

'I'll call Sarge now. He went out to have another chat with Murphy.' O'Connell lifted the desk phone and dialled. 'Do you know where the Thompsons are now?' He spoke as he waited for the call to connect.

'No. I've been busy chasing down Tom and Luke, but I overheard them arguing outside the Motel yesterday.'

'That's pretty standard in such a stressful situation.' O'Connell tapped his fingers as he waited for Sergeant Mackenzie to pick up his call.

'Yes, but they have also borrowed Marj's ute. I'd like to know where they are going with it.'

'You and me both. You follow up on that police check from overseas.'

'On it.' Jenny crossed to the front counter computer.

O'Connell hung up. 'Not answering.'

'Should we be worried?'

'I don't think so. Reception is rubbish out there. I'll try the Murphy's place.'

'I'll call Penny at the forensic lab and find out if they have anything else to add to the report yet. Nothing's come up online.'

'The wheels turn slowly Williams.' O'Connell pressed numbers on the desk phone. 'You'll need to learn a bit of patience I'm afraid.'

Jenny smiled. She never claimed patience was her forté. 'I'm working on it.'

Grabbing the mouse of the main counter computer, she spurred it to life with a vigorous shake. Checking the station email she found nothing about their police record request, not that she seriously expected anything. Anyone with a police record would be unlikely to get a holiday visa into the country.

She returned to her earlier internet stalking to learn more about the Thompson family. The sound of O'Connell's voice told her he got through to her boss, but she was focussed on discovering more about Beth's parents. Why stay in Coober Pedy? Why not kick up a fuss and call for a detective?

Jenny sighed as page after page of images of Beth Thompson in full pageant persona fuelled Jenny's desire to find out what happened to that eleven-year-old girl, all those years ago.

After nearly a dozen pages, Jenny's finger hovered over her mouse button, ready to click *Next*, but stopped.

Finally, a photo of someone else in the Thompson family appeared. Trent Thompson appeared at least twenty years younger. His uniform hung loose on his lean frame, as though it belonged on someone broader, heavier set.

His chest bore a row of medals, none of which Jenny knew anything about. Her military background was zero and her knowledge of US military was even further limited. Looking up, she saw Philips returning to the office, a ceramic mug that read *#1 Dad* in his hand, bringing the waft of instant coffee with it.

'Hey Philips, O'Connell. Do either of you know anything about US military?'

Both men turned, Philips frowned before shaking his head. O'Connell rose from his seat, strode to the front counter and peered over Jenny's shoulder, a crease on his brow as he scanned her screen.

'My dad was a military buff. A little obsessed over it to be honest, but he was particularly fixated with the US military. What do you need to know?'

'Looks like Trent Thompson served. Not sure it's relevant to our investigation, but do you know what these medals are for?' Jenny clicked on the photo, enlarged it and zoomed in on the medals on the young soldier's chest.

'Back up a bit.' O'Connell tapped the screen. 'Zoom in on the arm band first.'

Jenny obliged, noting a burgundy and gold insignia that resembled a snake curled around a sword with wings.

'That's US Medical Corps.'

Jenny looked from the screen to O'Connell's face and back, her eyes narrowed. 'He was a doctor?'

'It appears so.'

'Our records show he is a stock broker.'

'He might have resigned when he left the military?' Philips sipped his coffee.

'I'll see if I can find out why he isn't practising anymore.' Jenny clicked a new window open on her browser. Her mind was humming now, adrenalin kicking into high gear.

'Anything new on the mother?' O'Connell calmly returned to his desk and Jenny wondered how he wasn't pumped with the new information?

'Nothing. She appears to be a career pageant mum. I've not even been able to find a picture of her graduating class, where she went to school, nothing.'

'I managed to reach Sarge at Murphy's place. He's heading back to town soon, but won't get in until late. I told him about your interviews and Gavin. Hopefully he's got some information on where we can find Gavin, but he said Murphy hasn't seen him for a while. He's been unreachable.'

'Tom said he was working away.' Philips put his empty mug down on the counter.

'Murphy should know that. Or maybe he knows exactly where his son is but isn't telling us.' Her gut tumbled around telling her Murphy knew more than he was sharing.

'Gavin has always been a little simple. Works on the property from time to time but when Murphy gets tired of him, he takes a stint working as a truck driver at the mines,' O'Connell said.

Jenny waited, knowing that what was coming next wasn't going to be good news.

'Murphy tried to contact him at the mines. He's been missing, took off from his swing when Beth's body was found. Apparently, he hasn't called in at the family property.'

'We only have Murphy's word on that.' Jenny crossed her arms over her chest.

'I'm sure Sarge has considered that.' Jenny gawked at O'Connell a moment, wondering if challenging his idealistic thought was worth it. He was a smart guy. Surely he was asking himself the same questions? Murphy and her boss were obviously mates. *Damn, local policing was hard work.*

O'Connell carried on before she could decide a challenge was worth it. 'You and Philips call it a day. There's nothing much going on around town. The roads are only just being reopened to general traffic and we aren't going to solve this case this afternoon.'

'I still have to call Penny and see if she has any updates on the forensic front.'

'Okay.' O'Connell's tone said *if you have to,* but Jenny couldn't just let the matter drop because the weekend was coming up.

At the same time, tomorrow was Saturday and Nev was taking her out to meet his uncle. Jenny was hoping with all her heart that the indigenous tracker could shed some light on her family mystery.

Picking up the office phone at the counter, Jenny dialled the Adelaide Forensic Lab. The phone rang longer than she was hoping. Just as she was about to hang up, the line connected. A breathless voice answered.

'Forensics.'

'Penny. You sound like you ran a mile.'

'I was in the loo.' She continued to draw long deep breaths for a few more seconds.

'Are you on your own today?'

'No, but it's been busy.'

'Sorry to put the pressure on. Any updates on our case?'

Jenny heard keys tapping on the lab computer. 'I saw an update pop up today on Doc's report.'

'Nothing has come up our end yet.'

'It's probably still undergoing internal review, but.... let, me see.' A few seconds passed. 'Yep, here it is.' Another silence followed.

'What is it?' Jenny could picture Penny's frown with the long, extended pause.

'That's interesting. Doc says a few of the breaks in Beth's bones are old.'

'Like older than the six years she's been missing?'

'I..., just let me...., yeah. It's complex but there are growth plates and if a fracture occurs in a growth plate, in a younger person, it can cause abnormalities in the limb. Your victim has more than one of these stemming from multiple fractures. She also has other indicators that would suggest these fractures are all quite dated.

'Her abductor probably didn't cause the breaks then? That's if there ever was a kidnapper.'

'Doesn't look like it. We've also got a preliminary report on the baby. Indicators from bone analysis show it was premature or malnourished in utero.'

'That's horrible. The poor girl.'

'Whoever kidnapped her, wasn't exactly taking very good care of her.'

'Thanks Penny. I'll let the team here know. If I get some DNA from the possible father, can your lab put a rush on the report?'

'I'll try, but you know how long DNA takes to process. Could be months.'

Jenny sighed. 'Yeah. I know the drill. Thanks Pen. I'll catch you later.'

'Catch ya.' Penny hung up. Jenny placed the receiver down slowly, her mind running the information through again.

'Sir.' O'Connell peered up over his new reading glasses. 'Penny said the fractures we thought Beth Thompson sustained after her abduction, appear to be older than that.'

O'Connell removed his glasses, rubbed the bridge of his nose and put them back on, peering over the top at Jenny. 'Any medical reason why she would have sustained multiple fractures as a child?'

'Not that Penny or Doc Holbrook have discovered. She has no medical condition. Beauty pageant contestants aren't usually into gymnastics and such. But I'll check with her school to make sure.'

'And then there is the fact the fractures don't seem to be attended to properly.'

'Yeah, but that doesn't make sense either. If Mr Thompson was a doctor, then why wouldn't he set his daughter's broken bones himself?'

'Philips!' He was half way out the door, backpack on one shoulder, head down.

'Sir?'

'Go with Williams and find out if anyone has seen Marj's ute around town. Let's get a time line of where the Thompsons have been travelling. I want to know where they've been, who they've seen, even what they ate for dinner.'

'Yes Sir.' Philips gave Jenny a withering look. He was so close to an early finish on a Friday.

'Sorry.' Jenny whispered as he tossed his backpack into his locker and they retrieved their utility vests.

Chapter 26

Jenny precariously juggled three cups of coffee in her left hand, her chin holding them in place as she gently pushed the station door open, her eyes on the paper cups.

Philips noticed her, lifted the counter-top and rushed forward, just as the top coffee cup unseated itself and teetered on the verge of a coffee catastrophe.

'Thanks. I got one for you today.' She smiled at the shake of Philips' head. She would convert him to real coffee if it was the last thing she did before solving her family mystery and moving back to civilisation.

As she thought about Melanie and her aunt, she was reminded of her own family. There had been only a handful of calls to her parents since she moved. Her dad made it abundantly clear he didn't agree with her taking the transfer. But she needed to call him and her uncle Pete in any case.

'You know I only do instant.'

'Good thing I like real coffee then.' Sergeant Mackenzie grabbed the cup Philips rescued from certain disaster earlier.

'Sarge?'

'Don't look so surprised Williams.'

Jenny shut her mouth. Her boss was often absent, causing her to worry that he may have relapsed into his drinking. She knew very little about the Sergeant's history, but she did know the death of his daughter sent him spiralling into self-destruction.

'Report!' Sergeant Mackenzie sat on the edge of O'Connell's desk, sipping the coffee he seized from Philips. She was thankful she chose today to try and convince Philips to go with real beans.

'Why don't you brief him on what you know Williams? O'Connell smiled as she handed over the coffee.

'Yes Sir.' She took a sip of her own brew, followed by a deep breath as she launched into her report.

'Gavin Murphy is the likely father of Beth Thompson's baby, but you knew that. Forensics have revealed the infant was either born prem or was under-nourished in the womb. Either way, that doesn't look good for Gavin, who we are still yet to find.'

She stopped for another sip, another breath and continued.

'The Thompsons have been using Marj's spare Nissan to trek around town. We spent yesterday afternoon tracking their movements. They've been to the Opal Inn Bar where we found Luke and Tom the other day. That's who led us to understand Beth has been living with Gavin, seemingly of her own accord.'

'You're wandering Williams.' Mackenzie sipped his absconded coffee. 'Good coffee.'

'Thanks Sir. We split up yesterday afternoon and discovered they visited the bar, the service station by Marj's Motel and they were planning on heading out the William Creek Pub this weekend.'

'Who told you that?'

'Marj did.' Philips stirred his fresh instant coffee as he joined the conversation.

'Sir, Mr Thompson was in the Medical Corp. A qualified doctor. We're still awaiting official records. I'm only going from a photo of him in the local newspaper when he returned from service, complete with medals.'

'Anything else?'

'Yes Sir. The most important part. The forensic lab has confirmed that Beth Thompson's broken bones occurred when

133

she was young. Younger than the eleven years of age she was when she went missing.'

Sergeant Mackenzie stopped with his coffee halfway to his lips, a strange look crossing his face.

'What is it Sir?'

Mackenzie continued to take a long, slow drink, somehow sensing he might have given something away and now deciding if he should elaborate.

His nostrils flared, before he nodded to himself. 'Murphy claims he never knew anyone was living in the old shed.' Sarge drained his coffee before tossing the cup into the bin next to O'Connell's desk. 'He's holding something back, but I don't know what. I asked him if he knew where Gavin was. He said he didn't. I think he's telling the truth, but can't be sure.'

'Why not bring him in for a formal interview?'

'Williams, this isn't NCIS or some TV drama. Even if there was a reason, and the word of two drunken louts from the mining firm that Gavin works with occasionally isn't, we aren't in the city here. This is a small town. Murphy lives nearly two hours away and if we dragged him in, it will be rumour-mill central.'

'I get it Sir, but a woman is dead. Her baby too. Sure, she died in a horrible accident, but she's been missing for six years.' Jenny could hear her voice rising. She knew she was pushing her boss again, but he always wanted to sweep everything under a rug.

'Williams.' It was O'Connell's voice that she heard. His tone was calm, but Mackenzie's face wasn't and neither was his reply.

'You. In my office. Now!' The sergeant stormed to the back room, opened the door wide and beckoned her inside with a sinister look on his face. She glanced at O'Connell hoping for moral support, but found none.

Her stomach knotted as she ambled into the Sergeant's office. The curtains were still drawn, offering only a glimmer of light between the cracks. She needed to be in Coober Pedy. She needed this job to discover what happened to Melanie and Aunt Carolyn. She needed to keep her big trap shut.

'Sit!' the Sergeant pointed to the seat opposite him. 'Close the door first.' He seemed flustered.

Jenny turned, pushed the door closed and watched as Philips offered an encouraging smile. O'Connell only fixed his eyes on the screen in front of him.

She sat in the vinyl chair. The squeak it made, reflected the tight knot in her stomach that threatened to grip her throat. Her boss sat down heavily in the tall-back chair opposite. His fingers fidgeted, drawing circles on the desk blotter. Jenny's mind was so tense she found herself wondering what anyone needed a blotter for in the modern age of technology.

'When you first came here, I thought you were trying to gain a few rungs on the career ladder. Mackenzie's tone was calmer than she expected. 'You're a good officer Williams. That Tiffany case proved to me you have good instincts but you're new at this and to be bloody frank, you're an arrogant little shit for someone as green as you are.'

Jenny fought the urge to say something. Her sergeant grinned. 'Good to see you *can* learn when to keep your mouth shut.' She maintained eye contact, not wanting him to think his words stung.

'I've known most of these people for more than twenty years. I'll still be here long after you're on your way to a promotion in the big smoke. *While you're here Williams, you'll learn to do things my way.*'

Hot tears burned at the back of her eyes. She pushed the sensation away. The result made her body tense, her face tingle. The tears desperately wanted to be let loose.

'Yes Sir.' She knew there was no conviction in her statement. She didn't believe in tip toeing around the locals when major crimes were involved.

'I bet you did fingerprinting on old X-ray films when you were a kid.' The statement shocked her. She tried to hide it.

'Like I said, you've got natural instincts and I don't mind listening to any theory you come up with, but when it comes to interviewing some of the oldest and most respected members of our community, you'll spare me the high and mighty police academy rule book and leave it to me to decide the nature of said interviews.' He paused, watching her closely. 'Understand!' It wasn't a question.

'Yes Sir.'

'Okay, now back to the briefing, with everyone.' He nodded toward the door.

Chapter 27

The morning dragged on as Jenny searched for more information on the Thompsons. Her internet searches turned up nothing new and after running around in circles, she gave up.

'Any luck working out where Gavin is hiding himself?' She peered over the office desk computer toward Philips at the front counter.

'Nope. Sarge said he had a few ideas. He and O'Connell are heading out this afternoon to see if they can track him down.'

Philips glanced over his shoulder at the closed back office door. O'Connell and the Sergeant had been in there since the briefing finished half an hour ago.

'You okay?' Philips watched her, a deep crease in his forehead.

'Sure. Nothing I haven't dealt with a dozen times since I got here.'

'You are a bit headstrong you know.'

'So everyone keeps telling me.'

'I mean it as a compliment.' Jenny gazed up from the computer screen again to see Philips' frown replaced with a genuine smile.

'I know. Thanks.' She tapped a key to open the station email account. 'Yes!' She stabbed the air with her fist.

'What is it?'

'The Orange County Police have *finally* sent us a copy of the Thompson's file.'

'They have one then?'

'Seems so.' Jenny tapped the attachment open and scrolled as Philips joined her.

'That's weird.' Philips said what she was thinking.

'I'll print this out for Sarge and O'Connell.'

'What are you thinking?' Philips seemed perplexed as the printer kicked into action and the smell of hot paper and laser ink filled the air.

'A DUI doesn't exactly explain why Elizabeth Thompson might have run away from home.'

'You think she ran away now?'

'I don't know Philips. Something isn't adding up about her abduction.'

'We need to find Gavin.'

'You two need to knock off.' Both constables swung around to find Sergeant Mackenzie and Senior Constable O'Connell standing in front of Sarge's office. 'We'll go see if we can track Gavin down, but before you finish for the day, just check and see if the Thompsons are back in town or not.'

'I'll do it Sarge.' Jenny offered, handing him a copy of the police report.

'What's this?'

'The Orange County Police Report on the Thompsons Sir. It might explain why Doctor Thompson quit the profession.'

The Sergeant opened the file and skimmed through.' A whistle escaped his lips. 'DUI resulting in manslaughter.' He handed the file to O'Connell.

'Did he do time?' O'Connell read the file and answered his own question. 'A good behaviour bond. Must have friends in high places.'

'Extenuating circumstances the report says. P.T.S.D.' Jenny waited on her boss. This was what Philips found weird. The man seemed stable enough. Solemn, but stable.

'You're not buying it then Williams?' Sarge closed the file and handed it back to her.

'I don't know Sarge but there has been something niggling at the back of my mind since I met the Thompsons.

Then there was the argument outside the Motel. Trent Thompson's tone was calm, almost quiet and he has maintained his daughter ran away all this time.'

'Maybe he was molesting her and running away seemed the best explanation to keep his wife calm.'

'Maybe, but Suzanna Thompson is a pageant mum. Maybe she's being over dramatic claiming abduction, when in fact the kid just ran away from an overbearing mother.'

'Don't believe everything you see on TV Williams.' Sergeant Mackenzie jiggled his keys as he opened the door to leave. 'Lock up when you leave.'

'Yes Sir.'

'Text me if you find where the Thompsons are though.'

'Will do.'

Jenny opened her locker, and collected her backpack as Sergeant Mackenzie and Senior Constable O'Connell left the station. Philips joined her.

'You lock up. I'll check with Marj and see if she's seen the Thompsons. No one has told them about their daughter's pregnancy yet.' Jenny pulled her backpack from the locker and pushed it shut.

'Don't you think you should run that by the Boss first.'

'If it was my daughter I'd want to know.'

'They've been here long enough to have come to the station to sit with Sarge and talk about the case. They said they were here for answers, but they've not met with us once.'

'Exactly my point. I think I need to shake the tree a little bit and see what falls out. Giving them an update on the case might be a good place to start.'

'Just be careful.' Philips ushered her out as he flicked off the lights and pulled the front door closed.

'Nev is meeting me for lunch at the Motel. Then we'll head out to visit his uncle in the community.'

'What for?'

Had she let too much slip? 'Just curious.' She rushed to come up with an excuse when she didn't need to. 'I visited the cave painting on Nick's property recently and got a bit of a bug about the Indigenous history.'

'You two are getting close.' Jenny laughed aloud.

'Nev and Tim are just mates.'

'I meant Nick Johnston.'

'That's none of your business.' Jenny grinned and Philips chuckled.

'Dianna keeps asking me why you're not dating. At least now I can tell her you're saving yourself for Nick.'

'Piss off.' Jenny slapped Philips on the arm gently.

'He's a nice guy. You could do worse.'

'I'm not interested in a relationship Philips, and I don't know why I'm even talking to you about this stuff.'

'Because we're friends and you *should* be interested in a relationship. There is more to life than work, so much more.'

Jenny thought about Philips' son Tommy with his thick mop of blonde hair and tried to picture if she would ever have kids or not. It was so much easier for guys. They could have kids young and go back to work, but that was a huge sacrifice for a woman. They were torn between career and kids every day. Some women were born to be mums. Others were driven toward a career. In her case, that career was finding the truth about what happened to Melanie and Aunt Carolyn.

Thinking of family made her want to call her dad. She still didn't understand why he was so against her taking the job in Coober Pedy. Surely he was keen to find out what happened to his sister-in-law and niece and even more so, Uncle Pete should have been stoked she was trying to uncover the mystery.

Her mum always seemed to just want to change the subject. The more she thought about it, the more she wondered if she might have missed something all those years ago. *Did Aunt Carolyn just leave Uncle Pete and take Melanie with her?*

'See you Monday unless there is a major catastrophe of course.' Jenny waved as Philips got into the police Landcruiser and she crossed the road to the Motel.

'Like I said, tread lightly and stay safe.'

'You know me.'

'Exactly my point.' Philips closed the door to his vehicle. The motor kicked to life.

Jenny watched the car drive away before letting her mind wander back to her family. If Melanie left willingly, she would have made contact by now. No. Something horrible happened and this afternoon she hoped to find out how William Creek Station might be connected.

Jenny scoured the carpark as she passed Reception. No old burgundy Nissan. She peered into the office and caught sight of Marj hunched over her desk, her eyes downcast. It was an unfamiliar scene that made the hair on the back of her neck stand to attention.

'You okay Marj?' The woman glanced up with a start, her face passive, no smile, no twinkle in her eye.

'Sure luv.' Jenny wasn't convinced.

'The Thompsons out and about?'

'Yes.' The answer seemed too quick.

'Any idea where?'

'No.' *Too quick again.*

'Marj. What's going on?'

'Oh nothing luv. I just thought I was a better judge of character, that's all.'

'In what way?' Jenny strode into the office with an overwhelming urge to give the Motel owner a hug. 'Come on Marj. Spill.'

Marj bit her bottom lip as if she were trying not to say anything. 'I just thought Suzanna and I shared a connection. She was a mess when Elizabeth went missing and I spent a lot of time consoling her.'

'And what's changed?'

'I felt so bad about not recognising Beth's necklace the moment I saw it. I apologised to Suzanna.' Jenny waited patiently. She had never seen Marj so upset. 'She slapped me when I told her.'

'She what!' Jenny's adrenalin spiked instantly. No one could possibly have any reason to hit Marj, that was unthinkable. The woman was kind and funny and just lovely.

'Oh I understand it's my fault. She must be beside herself with grief now she knows Elizabeth is dead and I have no kids of my own and I should still know better than to think my apology would mean anything after everything that's happened.'

'Marj, even if you did tell her earlier about the necklace, it wouldn't have helped. Beth was already dead.'

'I know but I saw the necklace once before, since Elizabeth went missing and it totally didn't click then either.'

Jenny's pulse raced. 'Why didn't you tell the police, tell me?'

'I was so embarrassed I'd forgotten. I feel like my age is catching up with me. Maybe I've got dementia or something.'

'Marj, when or where did you see Beth's necklace?'

'I raided and old stash of opal and went to cash it in at Clancy's a while back. He had the necklace on his counter, well I think it was the same necklace. I didn't really think much about it until you showed me the photo of Beth and I kept thinking I'd seen it before.'

'Did you tell Mrs Thompson you saw it at Clancy's jewellery store?'

'I did. That's when she slapped me.' Marj touched her cheek reflexively.

'Not when you told her you failed to recognise it on Beth?'

She held her hand on her face as she considered her answer. 'No. Definitely when I told her I saw it in the jewellery shop. I think it was there for a repair.'

'Thanks Marj. You've really helped.' Jenny forced herself to stay calm. She wanted to turn and bolt out the door, but stopped at the doorway, her hand firmly on the frame to keep her grounded.

'How?'

'I'll let you know later.' She smiled, then scooted out the door. She jogged to the restaurant to catch Nev. Yanking the doors open, she spotted him leaning against the bar, beer in hand.

'Hey!' She called as she rushed toward the bar. 'I'm going to be late for lunch. I have to check something out first.'

'But I'm starving.'

'I need to run a lead for work.'

'Don't you ever stop? Surely it can wait until Monday?'

'I don't think it can. I need to call in to Clancy's.'

'The opal broker place? They'll be shut after twelve on a Saturday.'

'Damn!' Jenny let out an exasperated sigh, her shoulders slumped with disappointment. Trent Thompson was ex-military, sure he was medical corps but he was still trained. If he now believed someone abducted his daughter, then he could easily be tracking him down with some vigilante justice in mind.

She knew she needed to let Sarge know, but he would be out of range by now. Philips could get Clancy to open his store but Sarge was adamant she shouldn't ruffle the local's feathers.

'Damn.' She said again, almost hopping from one foot to the other with uncontained energy.

Nev watched her over the rim of his beer a moment. 'Look, let's grab a quick bite from the bakery, do a drive by Clancy's on the way to the Community and if he's open, we'll call in.'

Nev had no idea how important this could be and she wasn't about to make him privy to a police investigation, but she was thankful he was willing to forgo his lunchtime steak to put her mind at ease.

'Thanks. Let's go. I better drive though.' She watched him down his schooner of beer and snatched the keys from the bar before he could protest.

He reached for them but caught a glimpse of her expression and put the now empty beer glass down and his hands up in surrender.

'Okay, but you don't know the way.'

'How many beers have you drunk?' She watched Stan behind the bar to see if he would back up the Doctor.'

'Just the one.' Stan nodded with a grin.

She smiled and tossed the keys back to him. 'Let's go then.'

Nev rolled his eyes at Stan before trundling after the constable. 'Do you want to change first?'

Jenny observed her uniform and sighed. 'I'll change in the car.'

Nev's grin grew wider.

'While you keep your eyes on the road.' She waggled her finger at him.

'Of course.' Nev agreed and Stan chuckled aloud. 'Today just keeps getting better and better.' He raised his thick brown eyebrows Groucho style at the barman.

'Oh shut up!' Jenny pushed the restaurant door open and almost slammed it in Nev's face.

Chapter 28

'Okay, you were right.' Jenny wriggled out of her work slacks and into a pair of denim shorts. The moisture was drying up, but the air was stiflingly humid and Nev's car air-conditioning was barely reaching the back seat.

She watched him adjust his rear-view mirror. 'You better be adjusting that up so you can't see the back seat or I'm going to have to arrest you for indecent behaviour.'

'I'm not the one taking her clothes off in the back seat.' Nev grinned and Jenny could see his face in the mirror, answering her question.

'Perv.' She pulled her shorts on and slipped a tank top on over her sports bra. 'I can't believe Clancy was already gone for the day. Doesn't anyone have a work ethic in this place?'

'Miners' hours aren't like the rest of us. They come in early, when it's cool, then they head back underground during the heat of the day. Clancy doesn't do tourist work.'

'I'll text Philips to see if he can call in tomorrow and chase up a lead.' Jenny slid into the front seat, ignoring the fact she should have her seatbelt on. She told herself that bush road rules were flexible and to an extent they were. The roads weren't exactly busy with traffic. Kids could get away with more in the bush, and they often did.

'Do you want to share?'

'Can't, but probably best I don't. This is a weird case and it's ongoing.'

'Fair enough.' Nev changed down a gear, slowed for one of the town's only GIVE WAY signs, then sped up through the intersection as Jenny snapped her seatbelt in place. 'Uncle's looking forward to meeting you.'

Jenny expected Nev to put up more of a fight, but was thankful he didn't. 'Does your Uncle have a name?'

'Uncle.'

'Really!'

'It's a long story, but traditional culture prohibits using the name of a deceased tribal member. This gets complicated because sometimes mourning periods last a long time.'

Jenny nodded but failed to understand how this related to Nev's uncle's name, but she said nothing.

'Well Uncle's name was the same as a deceased family member way back… well actually I don't know how far back but anyway, years went by and Uncle decided it was easier not to use a first name and now we all just call him Uncle. Even community who aren't actually direct family.'

'Your uncle is an Elder. Right!'

'Yeah. He's known by pretty well everyone in the Community.'

'Where does that put you in the Community?'

'Indigenous culture doesn't have the same hierarchy as some might think. Just because my Uncle is an Elder, doesn't mean I should or will be.'

'Do you want to be?'

Nev changed gears as the Subaru Brumby turned onto the Sturt Highway heading South. He didn't speak for a minute and Jenny wondered if he was ignoring her or didn't want to answer the questions.

'Sorry if I'm being nosy.' She scanned his face.

'No, it's a good question. One I can't answer to be honest. I'm a kid of two nations. White education and father, Indigenous mother and upbringing.'

'You're the ideal person to be an Elder then.'

'Maybe.'

Jenny couldn't be sure, but she was aware Nev wasn't telling her everything, but she could hardly complain. There was a lot about her past she kept from him too.

'So you haven't really explained why you want to talk to Uncle.'

Jenny glanced across at Nev. 'No. Sorry. You're right. I haven't.' She skirted around the reason because Nev hadn't asked her directly. She planned on telling him the truth, but then his Uncle went walk-a-bout on Country for the past few weeks and only recently returned to the Community.

'I thought it was just curiosity about First Nation stuff at first, but that's not it, is it?'

Jenny considered how to answer the question. 'I'm finding the Indigenous history really interesting, but you're right, it's not why I want to see your uncle. You said he mentioned a curse on the William Creek Station.'

Nev didn't push. He kept his eyes on the road as they navigated a turn off the highway, onto a corrugated dirt track. The car started to shudder as the wheels rolled in an out of the ruts. She thought he would slow down, but instead, he dropped back a gear and accelerated, pushing the vehicle to skim over the bumps, smoothing out the ride.

'My cousin and aunt went missing my last year of high school and William Creek Station is the last place they were seen.' While not substantiated by anyone except Nick's worker Ed, Jenny's gut told her that's where Melanie was before she disappeared.

'And you're dating Nick to find out what happened to them?' Nev kept his eyes on the road.

'I'm not dating Nick. He's been helping with my enquiries.'

'I don't think he knows that.' Nev grinned, giving her a sideways glance.

Jenny ignored the comment. She wasn't sure what Nick did or didn't know about their friendship, but she wasn't about to tell Nev that they were investigating Nick's dad's supposed suicide and that Nick probably didn't know she existed other than that.

'So you never heard from your family after William Creek?' Nev must have read something on her face to change the subject so quickly. For a cop, she was terrible at bluffing sometimes.

'No.'

'I'm sorry.'

'They are the reason I'm here. I've waited years for an opening in the Coober Pedy area.'

'I'm not sure that's what most cops in their mid-twenties would be pining for.'

'I'm not most cops.' Jenny didn't look at Nev. Her eyes were focussed on a sprawling group of brick and metal buildings up ahead. A tall chain fence surrounded the area like a military compound.

'I'm beginning to realise.'

Nev slowed the vehicle as the chattering from road ruts returned. A large square sign with orange and brown traditional artwork announced the Umoona Community. A sticker in the bottom right-hand corner depicted bottles, inside a circle with a cross over the middle. The words *No Alcohol* sent a clear message to visitors and residents alike.

Jenny opened the door to a wave of heat. Early afternoon sun pelted down from a cloudless sky, baking every inch of red dirt that surrounded them. The heat haze on the horizon danced hypnotically as beads of sweat popped instantly on her skin.

'Get ready to be overrun.' Jenny frowned but there was no time to ask a question as kids in brightly coloured basketball shirts and shiny track pants bounced excitedly from various directions. The melodic sound of the indigenous language bubbled out of four or five bright smiling faces all at the same time.

'This is Jenny.' Nev tried to introduce her. More chatter erupted as the children grabbed her arms and hauled her inside the gate and on towards a large open shed by a red dirt basketball court. A modern brick building stood out amongst various tin clad structures.

An older man called out loudly in a mix of traditional language and English. The children giggled, then scattered. A football appeared seemingly from nowhere. Within seconds, the mass of giggling children moved like a swarm of bees out onto the playing field, dust rising as they kicked the ball around.

'Uncle.' Nev embraced the hunched man with grey hair and even greyer beard. 'This is Jenny. The new constable I told you about.'

'Welcome.' An earnest smile revealed a missing front tooth amongst otherwise straight, white teeth.

'Pleased to meet you Sir.'

'Uncle, everyone, they call me Uncle.' The smile broadened.

'Uncle.' Jenny instinctively dipped her head awkwardly, like she was meeting a Prime Minister, or a Royal or a Police Chief!

'Come. Eat.' The Elder wore long pants with a thick flannelette shirt. Jenny wondered how the locals never seemed to notice the searing heat like she did. The sun belted down, scorching everything in the desert all week, trying desperately to dry it out after the heavy rain ceased, but still the air was thick with moisture.

'I'm good. I grabbed lunch before I left.' Jenny's visions filled with raw witchetty grubs and burnt kangaroo tail. Her mental imagery reminded her of the *Indiana Jones* movie where the girl faints when the local Maharaja serves up the monkey heads.

Nev chuckled as though he understood what was going on inside her head. Maybe he did.

'I could kill a hot dog Uncle.'

'If you're having hotdogs, I might be persuaded.' Jenny grinned sheepishly. Uncle grinned and waved his hand to lead them under the shade structure. She fought the urge to jump straight into why she came today. This was Nev's family, his heritage. She told herself to embrace the experience, absorb what she could of aboriginal culture.

Her butt barely hit the long wooden bench before two women came from the brick building nearby. One was short and plump, the elastic in the bodice of her brightly coloured floral dress stretched, but she wore it proudly.

The second woman was younger. Tall and slim with stunning dark brown eyes and full lips. She didn't smile. Her eyes were downcast, shy even.

Three ice-cold cans of cola dripped with condensation. Jenny resisted the urge to reach out and grab one instantly, but when a platter of hotdogs with tomato sauce and mustard bottles was put down right in front of her, she almost laughed aloud.

Giving Nev a questioning gaze yielded no answer to her unasked questions. How on earth did he know they would have hotdogs ready?

Nev reached for one, loaded it with both sauces and virtually inhaled half of it before realising he should be playing host. 'Sorry.' He mumbled between chews. 'Uncle.' He swallowed hard. 'Jenny wants to hear the story of the William Creek Station Curse.'

Nev said it like it was a commonly told story, but the sudden expression on his uncle's features said there was nothing common about it.

The old man shook his head and waved his hand like he wouldn't speak of it at all and for a moment Jenny thought they might have travelled all this way for nothing.

'Not here.' He watched the children playing nearby. The dust rose around their feet as one boy kicked the ball across the yard and three more ran to intercept.

'Sorry Uncle.' Nev seemed suddenly subdued. Did he know the story? Did he even need to bring her out here to speak with his uncle?

They ate as they discussed Nev's work, general community news including the latest new addition to the family, issues with alcohol and glue sniffing in the young and how Nev should be considering the Elder's council before it was too late.

Jenny could see Nev was torn. She didn't understand much about his culture – only what she learnt at school which wasn't much at all. Now, the Indigenous communities in Australia were finally being heard, but was it too late?

'Come.' Uncle stood, brushed off a few crumbs from his beard before ambling away from the kids toward the front gate.

For a minute Jenny thought they were going to be leaving without the story she came to hear, but Uncle stopped outside Nev's car.

He spoke in his own language and Nev translated.

'It's Sorry Business.' Nev said, his tone telling her this was news to him as much as to her.

'Not common knowledge anymore. I was a boy,' he held his hand at mid-thigh height, 'when it happened.'

The old man slipped into English. 'Johnstons are cursed.'

'What do you mean? I thought the station was cursed?' Nev's brow creased.

'White Fellas,' he checked over his shoulder to make sure no one was listening, 'they said one of the community took old Johnston's daughter.'

The English was gone again and Nev wasn't translating. His expression was worried. Nev never look worried.

'Why haven't you told me before?' Nev asked when Uncle appeared to finish his story. Jenny wanted to scream for them to speak English, but she knew that was wrong. This was Nev's Uncle's story and he could tell it in any language he wanted to.

'Ancient history. Sins of the father.'

Nev was silent a moment. 'Why now?'

'She asked.' He pointed to Jenny. 'No one asked before.' His smile was back. Whatever the *Sorry Business* was, he didn't seem to hold a grudge over it.

'And you worked there?'

Uncle shrugged. 'History. Like I said. Nick and Sam, good kids.'

And their father? Jenny squirmed as she struggled to keep the question to herself. The few snippets she got of the story only raised more questions. But Nev wasn't about to explain it all to her again in English, not now.

'I always thought you were just joking about a curse.'

Uncle shrugged again. 'Maybe it's broken.'

'You think so?' Nev sounded dubious. 'Thanks for the hotdogs Uncle.' He turned to open the driver's side door.

153

'Yes, thank you for seeing me.' Jenny's chest tightened with frustration. She didn't need to be here. Nev could have asked the question and she could have saved herself half a day and been with Nick now, instead of standing out in the middle of nowhere. She put her hand on the door handle – a row of bright clothing and smiling faces waved at her beyond the gate and the tightness in her chest fell away.

She got in as Nev slipped in behind the wheel. He fired up the engine and they drove down the dirt road, the rattle of the vehicle over the corrugations the only sound as they remained silent.

She gazed out the window, watching the red earth and native grasses glide by. Her mind emptied, her anxiety abated as she realised the trip wasn't a waste of time. The smiling faces came to mind. She was fortunate to have met a special member of the Ngurabanna Nation and had a glimpse into Nev's childhood.

A simple life. Where kids could be kids and families spent time together. Her own childhood was good, but she grew up working. Cutting hay, carting hay, milking cows and going to school. She saw little of her parents as they strived to build a legacy. A legacy she and her brothers walked away from – to pursue their own lives.

She suddenly understood Nev's dilemma more clearly. Now she just needed to get the story she came for.

Chapter 29

Jenny wanted to push Nev, but the set of his jaw told her he needed time to digest what his Uncle shared with him.

Sorry Business! Her understanding of what that meant was only basic, but she needed more details. Facts. Something that could help her solve the mystery around her aunt and cousin's disappearance, and maybe even Nick's dad's death.

'I don't think Uncle's story is going to help you find out what happened to your cousin and aunt.' Nev spoke quietly, his tone serious.

'Maybe not, but I'd like to be the judge of that if you'll let me.' Nev didn't speak and Jenny became aware the story must have been very disturbing. Nev was a smart guy. Always cheery. Nothing much seemed to faze him, but his reaction and his behaviour now, made her want to tread lightly.

Nev slowed down at a crossroads, checked both ways and turned left. Jenny saw a signpost pointing toward William Creek as she recognised their location. They were back on the Coober Pedy, William Creek Road, not far from where Beth's accident occurred.

'Melanie, that's my cousin. She sent me a postcard from Coober Pedy saying they were planning a trip to the William Creek Station. Nick's dad's records say they never arrived. Nick's worker, Ed, says he saw Mel with Nick's dad.'

Jenny watched the scenery fly by through the side window, aware of Nev's lingering gaze.

'You believe Nick's dad was involved with your family disappearing?'

'I don't know what I believe.' *Nick's dad killed himself. Or someone did it for him. Both could be motivated by the fact people disappeared. Even Nick's mum went missing.* 'I just thought your uncle's story might shed some more light on what might have happened out there.

'The Sorry Business was from when Uncle was a boy. Way before Nick's dad was in charge of the station.'

'It could still be relevant.' Jenny pushed.

'Uncle said that someone in the Johnston family shot and killed at least a half dozen of the local Ngurabanna people.'

Jenny gasped. 'That's horrible.'

'Times were different back then, but Uncle doesn't know the full story. Only that it was something to do with one of the Johnston women and a young aboriginal man.'

'That sounds ominous.'

'I wish we kept better records. Handing stories down verbally can be like Chinese Whispers.'

'Nick's family might have something documented? Diary entries maybe?'

'And what. I'm just going to walk up to Nick Johnston and say, hey mate, apparently your mob killed a heap of mine way back when and I'd like details if you have them!'

Jenny bit her lip. 'Yeah. Maybe not.'

'It's too long ago to have anything to do with your family though. Uncle just said that Nick's dad's death was the work of the curse. He reckons the family was cursed since they killed on Country.'

'And you believe him?'

'I don't subscribe to the idea of a curse, but violence can run in a family – in their genes.'

'That can be true, but without the details, we can't know for sure what set off the attack.' A muscle twitched at the edge of Nev's jawline. 'Not that there is ever any excuse for outright murder. That's not what I meant, but hot heads and systemic violence are two different things. That's all I meant.'

Nev didn't speak for a good minute. Jenny watched the rugged landscape fly by as the four-wheel drive bounced over the corrugations left in the dried mud. Her muscles ached as she tried to keep her seat, every fibre of her body stiffly resisted the jolting momentum.

'You're right. I've known Nick and Sam for years. Neither has a violent streak that I've seen. I'm just shocked by Uncle's story and surprised I've never heard it before now. I can't believe he's kept it to himself. I can't believe he used to work at the station after everything that happened!'

Jenny didn't know what to say. Nev spoke into the silence. 'Did your text get through to Danny earlier?'

She welcomed the change of subject. Reaching over into the back seat, she retrieved her backpack and pulled out her mobile. There was no signal now, but the last text she sent went through successfully and Danny's reply was an emoji.

'Yep.'

'You sure you don't want to tell me about the case you're working on? We've still got a bit of a way to go before we arrive at Nick's place.'

'I really can't say much.' She put her phone back in the backpack and left it at her feet.

'Is it about the girl that died last Friday? I thought that was an accident.'

'It was.' She wasn't going to give him anything. She couldn't. But maybe he could give her something. 'Do you know Gavin Murphy at all?'

Nev glanced at her out the corner of his eye, but his focus shifted back to the road quickly as a huge, red kangaroo bounded into their path. He swerved to the right as the roo sprang up over six feet into the air, clearing the bullbar of the four-wheel drive by a whisker.

'Shit! That was close.' Jenny's fingers were embedded in the vinyl seat. Her pulse raced in her ears. Taking a slow breath, she released it and watched over her shoulder to see the kangaroo bounce off across the red desert.

'It's all the water sitting around on the side of the road. It makes the grass grow and the roos come in to feed as the sun gets lower and the day gets cooler.'

'Are you going to be okay driving home later?'

'I won't stop long at Nick's place. I'll get back on the road and stop over at the pub. Mrs B. loves feeding me. It's a shitty time to be out driving when there are so many roos around.'

They drove on toward the Oodnadatta Track intersection. Jenny let Nev settle back into driving before asking the question again.

'Oh yeah, sorry. I've treated Gavin. Don't know him all that well. He's quite a few years younger than me. Why?'

'Oh, it's just that accident you were talking about happened out near Murphy's property and Gavin's been out of contact for days so we haven't been able to ask him if he knew the victim at all.'

'You still don't know who she is?'

'We do now.'

'So why do you need to speak with Gavin?'

'We probably don't. Just thought it was strange that no-one seemed to know where he was.'

'Nice kid but not the sharpest tool in the shed by any means.'

'Yeah. I heard that.' They slowed to turn onto the Oodnadatta Track and head to William Creek Station. The William Creek Hotel was to the right, only a few kilometres up the road. A new dark blue Landcruiser utility was kicking up a red dust cloud in the distance, but otherwise the road was deserted.

Nev turned left as Jenny let her mind wander. It was a good fifteen minutes to Nick's place if you counted the track into the property. She wondered what reception she might get on this visit to the old homestead. Nick was all smiles in the chopper, until they found the tin shed where Beth's baby was buried in a shallow grave.

All the blood on the mattress was foetal, or Beth's mixed with amniotic fluid from giving birth. *She must have been terrified, all on her own like that.*

Now they knew that her historical broken bones were from her childhood and the very same parents who could be responsible were out bush somewhere in Marj's old burgundy Nissan trying to do what?

Damn you Clancy.

If the jeweller, come opal buyer were open, she would already have had her answer about who brought the necklace in for repair.

The vibration of a cattle grid jolted her from her daydream. The weather-worn sign greeted her. Nev gave her a quick smile as they passed under the overhanging sign.

'You were off with the fairies.'

'It's been a long day. Thanks for bringing me out here.'

'I think Nick would have come and got you in a flash.' Nev's grin reminded Jenny of the little aboriginal kids at Umoona.

'You could have let him.'

'That would take all the fun out of it. I'd miss the look on his face when I rock up and he has to deal with the fact that I've had you all to myself all afternoon.'

'You're such a stirrer.'

'You better believe it.' The homestead came into view and Jenny was excited to see Nick standing outside the double entrance doors waiting for her.

Chapter 30

'Hey.' Jenny called as she reached back in the door to retrieve her backpack from the front floor.

'Hey yourself.' Nick jumped from the veranda. 'Long drive. You guys need a drink?' It was the friendliest Jenny had ever seen him.

'Nah mate. It's getting late. I'll head to the pub and crash there for the night. You two have fun.' Nev waved from the driver's seat with an expression that Jenny found hard to read. She knew Nev wanted to be more than friends but he seemed fine leaving her with Nick for the night.

Did that worry her? No! Of Course not.

Nick watched the beaten-up Subaru ute slide sideways in the dust as it drove around the circular driveway heading away from the William Creek Station Homestead. Watching Nev disappear made Jenny self-conscious. This was going to be the first time she stayed at the Homestead. The first time alone with Nick, that is if Sam, his little brother wasn't in.

'I downloaded your dad's file and brought you a copy.' She flung the backpack over her shoulder.

Nick ushered her inside. 'Cool drink first, then we can talk.'

Jenny followed him up the stairs to the long veranda, through the double front doors and down the hall to the back of the homestead where the kitchen opened out to a large extension. The spectacular view of the escarpment beyond never got old. The floor to ceiling windows allowed her to take in the scenery, enveloping her, reminding her of the day she saw the indigenous artwork, the green tinged valley full of cattle grazing and the serenity of that rock formation. The memory made her skin tingle.

Or was that Nick causing the strange sensation?

'Juice, wine or beer?' Nick opened the fridge.

'I could definitely do with a beer. Thanks.' She placed her backpack on the table before taking a seat. 'Is Sam home?'

'No. He's over at Mick's place, serving at the bar for a few hours, then they'll head out for some roo shooting I reckon.'

She was finally here, alone with Nick with his undivided attention, eager to solve the missing persons case that surrounded her aunt and cousin for nearly seven years and she wasn't sure if she was ready to go there. There were so many unanswered questions. Why did Ed say he saw Nick's dad with Melanie, but there were no records? Then there was the *Sorry Business* Uncle talked about. Was it relevant?

'You okay?' Nick placed the beer down on the table as the sun began to dip over the escarpment beyond. The sky was streaked with purple and yellow, the first stars twinkling into life.

'Sorry. Yeah, it's just been a crazy day. We've got an exceptionally curly case we've been working on.'

'You mean the hit and run that led you to Murphy's farm?' Jenny didn't say anything. 'Do you want to talk about it?'

'I'd love to but Sarge would be seriously pissed if I let anything important slip.' She pulled a file from her backpack. 'Besides, we've got your dad's case to look over.'

'And your family case too.' Nick sat down, took a swig of his beer then shuffled over closer on the timber bench seat to look over Jenny's shoulder as she opened the case file. The smell of his spicy aftershave made her toes curl and her stomach do summersaults.

'Okay. I took a look before I came out but it was super quick. Nothing jumped out but there are graphic photos in here.' She studied Nick, his face only a few inches from hers. 'Are you sure you want to look at this with me?'

Nick took another sip of his beer, followed by a long slow breath in and out. 'When dad died, I was away at Uni. I didn't see him, or anything of the scene. It was all cleaned up by the time I arrived.'

'If you're sure.' Jenny slowly opened the notes in case Nick changed his mind. He didn't. A photo of the very dining table they were sitting at appeared first. Nick's dad was slumped over the table. A pool of blood surrounded him. A rifle lay across the table, beneath his right hand.

The scene made Jenny's stomach churn. They were literally sitting in the same spot as Nick's dad when he died.

'That's dad's rifle.' His tone was calm.

Jenny pulled the medical report out and put it on top of the photo. Nick reached for the picture, placing it to the left side of the table in front of them. He continued to study it as Jenny read the report.

'This isn't a coroner's or medical examiner's report.' Nick drew his eyes away from the photo to look at the piece of paper in Jenny's hand. 'This is a doctor's report.'

'Like I said. The case was closed and dad's body was released for burial before I even got back from Adelaide.' His eyes wandered back to the photo.

'The doctor declared it suicide. Do you know who this guy is?' Jenny pointed to the signature and name on the file.

Nick rubbed his chin, then tapped his index finger on his lip. 'No. Maybe he was a temp. We get them in town sometimes.'

'I'll see if I can find out and speak to him. Nev might know who he is.' Jenny read on as Nick's gaze fell back on the photo of his dad. It wasn't healthy to stare at it but Nick seemed calm, relaxed even. Like he was trying to unravel a

163

puzzle as he considered it rather than reliving what must have been an horrific time in his life.

'No toxicology was done.'

'They probably saw this empty bottle and assumed dad was loaded.' Nick pointed to the empty bottle of scotch to the left of the scene on the table.

Jenny frowned. There was something just not right about the whole picture but she couldn't put her finger on it.

'No matter which way you look at this, it was a cockup. No autopsy, no tox screening. Someone just took one look at a gunshot victim and called the suicide card. Why?' Jenny gazed at Nick earnestly. It made no sense. 'There isn't even a gun residue test. Was your dad thought to be suicidal? Was he on anti-depressant medication?'

'Not that I know of. I didn't find anything in the house when I cleared mum and dad's room out.'

'We need to open this case up again, but I'm going to need to do some serious digging before I take this to Sergeant Mackenzie. I might run it by O'Connell first and see what he suggests.'

'Are you sure? I don't want to get you into any trouble.' Nick's voice was laced with concern.

Jenny was too annoyed to be concerned. Len Holmes dropped the ball on this one. Maybe it was because he was covering the sergeant's arse while he tried to sober up after his daughter's death, but either way, it was a crappy investigation.

'O'Connell is good value. He knows I'm investigating Melanie and Aunt Carolyn's disappearance. He'll be okay with it. I'll run it past him Monday.'

'I'd appreciate that.' Nick got up, put his empty beer bottle in a crate by the fridge and opened the fridge. Jenny thought he was going for another beer until he pulled out a plate with two steaks on it.

'Where are you at with your family mystery?' Nick opened the sliding glass doors at the rear of the living area. 'Grab a few more beers and bring them out the back. I need to throw these on the barbie.'

Jenny sculled the last mouthful of her beer, gently dropped the empty in the crate alongside Nick's before opening the fridge. With two beers in hand, she followed him outside. The sun was disappearing behind the escarpments, the air was cooling, the smell of eucalypts and mowed grass hung in the warm air.

'Here.' She screwed the top off the beer and handed it to him as he closed the lid on the barbecue.

'Thanks.' He reached for the beer, raised it to hers. The necks of the bottles chinked. 'Cheers.'

She smiled, sipped her beer then picked up the conversation. 'I've been going in circles. Only Ed ever saw Melanie here. Len Holmes' file on the case shows that no one else in town saw either of them. Then there is Mrs B. at the William Creek Pub who said they skipped out on their bill, which just isn't their style at all.'

'And my dad's records say they never arrived.'

'Yeah and that. Rebecca helps out with bookings now, right?' Jenny referred to the woman she met the first time she visited the Homestead. 'Who did them back when Melanie was seen here?'

'Rebecca was at Uni like me back then. Mum used to do the books, take the bookings and such, but dad kept the log of visitors.' Nick busied himself turning the steaks, but Jenny could see talking about his still missing mum was tough.

The idea of visitors gave Jenny an idea. 'Do you keep a visitor's book? You know, the type where people write how much they enjoyed their stay?'

Nick chewed his lip a moment. 'Not now, but we used to.'

'Do you still have them from back then?'

'Maybe. They'll be stored away in the cellar.' Smoke rose from under the barbecue hood. The smell of juicy steak made Jenny's stomach rumble softly.

'You have a cellar?'

Nick gave her one of his rare smiles. 'Yeah, it's haunted too. Want to check it out?'

'You're kidding right?' Jenny studied his face. It was hard to tell. She didn't believe in ghosts, but when someone said a place was haunted, it alluded to something horrible having happened in the past. It made her think of Uncle's story.

'We'll check it out after dinner. You can be the judge.' Jenny watched him pull a medium-rare steak off the barbecue onto a clean plate. 'You okay with medium-rare?'

Jenny nodded but all she could think about was Uncle's *Sorry Business* and the possibility that there might be real ghosts in Nick's cellar. Or worse. There could be more substantial evidence that put Melanie on Nick's property before she went missing.

Chapter 31

'Have you been down here much?' Jenny couldn't get the idea out of her head, that Melanie might have been held captive in the Johnston's cellar.

'Not much. It was used in the old days to keep food cool so it would last longer. Dad used to keep a small wine stash down here. A few bottles of Para Port. Probably worth a small fortune now, but I sold them off years ago to pay back some of the farm debt.'

'So your dad kept wine down here back then? Nothing much else?' Nick flicked a light. It did nothing to relieve the eeriness of the musty smelling cellar. The steak suddenly weighed heavily in her stomach, making it knot and convulse. She told herself to stop being stupid, but what if Nick's dad did hurt Melanie? What would that do to her relationship with Nick?

'He kept old farm records down here. Tax paperwork, guest books, that kind of thing, but I don't think we'll find any rare jewels or anything of worth.'

Jenny forced herself to ignore the oppressive darkness that waited in every corner of the old limestone cellar.

'What about diaries? Did your dad or mum keep a diary? Or your Grandad maybe?' Jenny was thinking of the *Sorry Business* now as much as her own family affairs. Old farms were treasure troves of family history and judging by the bookcases filled with ledgers, Nick's was no exception.

'Probably.'

'You've never gone through them?' Jenny wanted to slap some sense into him. So much history could be lost if he never bothered to read them.

'I've been pretty busy since my dad died and my mum disappeared.' Nick's tone wasn't defensive for a change.

Instead he sounded tired but Jenny knew he must miss his mum. Worse, the not knowing would be torture. She knew it would be for her if the roles were reversed.

'I get that, but I would have been head down reading this old stuff if I lived here.'

'You're a cop. It's in your blood.' Nick pulled a small flashlight out of his back pocket and flicked it on. Holding it between his teeth like someone out of a Jack Reacher spy thriller, he rummaged through piles of books and ledgers.

Dust rose, making a mist in front of the flashlight. Burgundy, green and blue bound books caught Jenny's eye, making her think of her mum and dad's big farm ledgers. They were always full of figures written in pencil so that dad could rub them out and change them if the tax didn't work out quite right at the end of the year.

'What's that?' Jenny saw a smaller book with flowers on the outside.

'I don't know.' Nick ignored it and carried on looking through the ledgers.

'Can I have a look?'

'Sure, but I don't think that's a visitor's book. It looks more like a diary or something.' Jenny reached for the book.

'No, but it looks interesting.' She placed the worn book with faded violets aside and kept looking for the guest books she hoped to find.

'Here.' Nick held up a stack of elongated books, all hard backed, all brown with a white diagonal corner on the front. 'This is them. These days we just use Trip Advisor.' He opened one and scanned the contents. 'Yep. These are the right books. We can take them upstairs and go over them.'

'Let's do it.' Jenny collected the flower adorned diary as she made her way back to the worn hardwood staircase. It rose sharply, more like a ladder, but the hairs on the back of her neck as she stood looking up into the light made her hurry her way to the surface.

Ten minutes later they were settled side by side at the dining table thumbing through the guest book from two thousand and six. 'This is the crew from the Birdsville Bash.' Nick's face broke into a rare grin.

Jenny studied the comments and double checked the date. 'July two thousand and six. Melanie would have been here in late September, early October.'

Nick flicked over a few more pages. There were multiple different colour inks and handwriting, but nothing jumped out at Jenny. She sighed loudly. Nick eyed her sideways.

'So she didn't sign the visitors book. That doesn't mean she never came.'

Jenny was surprised to hear Nick admitting his dad might have missed something. So far, all she heard was good things about Mr Johnston senior from his older son. Did his dad have a dark side?

'What was your dad like?'

Nick stayed silent a moment. Making a concerted effort to appear to be focussed on putting the visitors' log back in careful and accurate date order, but Jenny could see he was contemplating his answer.

'Tough old bastard, but I know he loved us. A lot!'

'Sounds like my dad. It was always mum with the hugs. Dad was all about tough love. Never hit me mind you, but he never let me get too close either.'

'They sound similar.'

'My Uncle Pete was the opposite when we were growing up. It was the weirdest thing. He was always there with a hug. Mel hated it. She would duck under his arm as he tried to pull her close. Pete is still always cheery – that is until I told him I was heading here.'

'Not impressed?' Nick pulled a ledger from another pile and opened it.

'No, neither was my dad. "Why give up a great career so close to home? You'll put your career on hold if you go bush like that." They didn't let up, either of them. My dad was so annoyed that he didn't even see me off on the plane.'

'That's a bit extreme isn't it?'

Jenny shrugged. It offended her at the time, but she chose to let it go.

'I put it down to being the only daughter. He was just being protective.'

Nick frowned at her. She could see questions hovering on his lips. But he said nothing. His eyes returned to the accounts ledger in front of him. Jenny followed his gaze, noting the dates in the left-hand column were all early October two thousand and six.

Nick ran his finger down the names and amounts column, looking for anything that could be a tour fee. He reached for the corner of the page as Jenny gasped.

'What?' He turned to her as she threw her hand on top of his harder than intended. The sensation wasn't exactly horrible, but it was certainly a little awkward.

'Sorry.' She snatched her hand away.

'Don't be.'

Was that because he liked her hand on his or because she was just stopping him from changing pages?

His eyes studied hers. She glanced away. 'I saw something.'

Nick took his hand away so he didn't obscure her view.

'That is Mel's handwriting. I'd stake my job on it.'

'This?' Nick pointed to an entry in pencil. The description was in some sort of code. Letters and numbers, no full name. 'I don't know what those letters mean. Maybe Rebecca would?' He checked his watch. 'We can ask her tomorrow, it's too late now.'

Jenny glanced at her watch. It was later than she thought. It was late enough that farmers were usually in bed. The idea of going to bed made Jenny blush slightly.

'Are you okay?'

'I'm fine. Thanks for asking. Why would Melanie be writing in your dad's ledger?'

'Mum's ledger. Mum did all the accounting.' Nick touched the ledger tenderly, as though it were his mum's arm or face.

Both his parents were gone and Jenny realised just how lucky she was for hers to still be alive. She needed to call them more.

'How about a nightcap? We can mull over all this info tomorrow, over breakfast.'

'I'll show you to your room first, then we can grab a port or rum and check out the stars.' Nick folded the corner of the ledger page before flipping it closed. As he got up, Jenny couldn't help being disappointed about having her own room for the evening.

Chapter 32

Jenny woke up with her phone buzzing on the bedside table. Surprised to see it even working this far out of Coober Pedy, she quickly answered it in case the line dropped out.

'Jenny here.'

'Jenny. It's Danny.'

'Hey. What's up?' Jenny wandered to the window in her underwear. Pulling the curtains aside, she saw Nick by the stables brushing down a taller than average brumby.

'I managed to get Clancy to phone me back after-hours last night. It was too late to bother you but I figured you'd be up bright and early on the station out there.'

Nick turned and saw her in the window. Smiling, he waved that he was coming in. Jenny wondered why he looked up to her window? Maybe he figured she would be awake by now?

'You there?'

'Yeah. Sorry. Reception is crap.' She lied. *Well it usually was.* 'What did he say?'

'Just what you expected. Gavin Murphy took that necklace in for repair.'

'Got him.' Jenny tucked her phone between her chin and her shoulder as she scrambled into her denim shorts. 'I'll grab breakfast. Then head out to see if Murphy knows where his son is now that we know he knew Beth Thompson.'

'Sarge and O'Connell are probably still out there. I think they were staying overnight.'

Jenny puzzled over what to do. 'Okay. You try Sarge or O'Connell on their mobiles and the police radio. Let me know if you don't get them, but don't call Murphy's home line. He'll know something is up if you do and if there is any evidence of Beth on their property, I don't want to tip them off.'

'Okay. Sounds like a plan. But what if I can't get them and then I can't get you again?'

'Call me at William Creek Station.'

'Right. Will do.' Philips hung up. Jenny rushed to put on her T-shirt before loading her toothbrush. As she brushed, she removed her uniform from her backpack, before stuffing all her other clothing back inside.

Placing her uniform on top just in case she needed to make her enquiries at the Murphy property instead of Sarge.

A few minutes later she followed her nose to the kitchen to find Nick making pancakes.

'Oh my god that smells divine. Why hasn't someone made you a househusband already?' Nick grinned, something which was usually rare but was becoming a little more consistent of late. She liked it.

Suddenly realising what she said, she blushed. It rolled off her tongue without thought. Something she might say to a friend, or one of her brothers, not a prospective boyfriend. Was Nick a prospective boyfriend? Where did that thought come from?

'Remember. My mum and Mrs B. tried.' Jenny recalled the story of how he and Mrs B.'s daughter Rebecca were expected to get married after university. Was it Nick's dad's death that changed that? Or did they never intend going through with it?

Rebecca would certainly say yes! Of that she was sure. It was obvious in the way the administrator of the Station glared at her the first time they met. With her long bouncy brown ponytail, pouting lips and stern frown.

'Speaking of Rebecca. Did you manage to get a hold of her at all?'

'Certainly did. We can take the ledger to her at the pub after breakfast. She's got a few hours on shift there looking after a big tour bus coming in, then she can check it over for us.'

'Thanks so much for helping out with this Nick.' Jenny took a seat in front of an empty plate laid out with cutlery.

'No. Thank you, for seeing if we can open up dad's case again.' He placed a large stack of pancakes in front of Jenny and smiled. 'Don't worry. I have no doubt you could eat them all, but if you struggle, Sam will be back soon to help us finish them off.'

'Oh thank goodness. My stomach might want that many, but I'm not sure I could handle the food coma to follow.'

Nick laughed in a way that made Jenny look sideways at him as he sat down opposite her. 'What?' she asked.

'Nothing.' He shook his head before loading his plate with two pancakes.

'No. What?' She loaded her mouth again, waving her fork at him as she pushed for an answer.

'Most women go on about carbs and their figure, but you just say what you're thinking and eat what you want.'

'And?'

'And I like it.' Nick put a forkful of food in his mouth and Jenny did the same.

As she swallowed, it occurred to her that she might need to ask Nick to take her to Murphy's place again. She didn't like the idea of mixing her personal investigations and Nick's friendship with her real work case, but he was her only transport today.

'After we've been to the pub, would you mind taking me out to Murphy's on official business again? Hopefully Danny has gotten through to Sarge or O'Connell, but if not, I might have to follow up.'

'Still can't tell me what this is about?' She shook her head. 'It's fine. I'd already planned the day off.' Jenny opened her mouth, not to say anything, but in sheer surprise. 'I know. You are having the weirdest effect on me Constable Williams. An afternoon and a whole day off. Unheard of.'

'Oh I don't think I can take the blame for this one. I think the idea of solving a decade old mystery is driving you stark raving mad.'

Nick laughed again. *I love that smile!* She fought the blush in her cheeks again. The curse of having Irish and Scottish heritage. The white skin went red at the slightest provocation.

The thought of a curse reminded her about the diary she found last night in the cellar. 'Oh. I forgot to ask.' Thankful for a change of subject she rushed on. 'That diary we found. Would you mind if I grab it for a few days and read it?'

Nick finished his pancake and reached for another. 'Be my guest. It looks like Gran's diary and she always told fantastic stories. Not sure how many of them were true, but you should find it interesting reading.'

'I look forward to delving into William Creek Station's deepest, darkest secrets.' She grinned cheekily, but deep down she hoped to uncover more about Uncle's *Sorry Business*. She realised it probably was nothing to do with her or Nick's dad's case, but it was another mystery that needed solving and Jenny now understood, she was born to solve mysteries.

Chapter 33

Nick opened the pub door and held it as Jenny entered. *Who said Chivalry was dead?*

'Thanks.'

Nick followed her toward the front bar which was a lot quieter than last time Jenny visited. She recalled how the place was crawling with busloads of tourists, but it was lunch time. Today, it was a smaller, quiet group for breakfast.

'I thought you were coming after I finished the bus load.' Rebecca scowled from alongside Mrs B. behind the long wooden bar. The walls were covered in currency notes from all over the world. From the ceiling hung hats with car manufacturer logos and branding of all types. Many were signed.

'We got an early start.' Nick pulled up a stool next to his and patted it for Jenny to take a seat. 'Can we grab two cappuccinos thanks? How do you have yours?'

'Do you have caramel syrup?' Rebecca nearly choked, Mrs B. chuckled and Nick outright laughed. Hard.

'Yes luv. We can find you some caramel syrup. Sweets for the sweet.' She hummed as she moved to the other end of the bar where the alcohol lined the shelves. 'How about Frangelico?'

'I might need to go on duty Mrs B., so I'll just have three sugars if you don't have caramel.'

'Found it!' Mrs B. called from under the back counter.

'Thank god for that. Three sugars would be harder to pour than caramel syrup.' Rebecca grumbled.

'Lucky you don't have to pour it then.' Nick nodded to Rebecca's mother who was loading the tall mug with syrup.

'Can you take a look at this for us?' Nick pushed the ledger closer to Rebecca and flipped it open to the page with the bent corner. 'Do you recognise what these initials and numbers mean? Mum trained you to take over the books.'

Rebecca pulled the ledger closer and studied it without any real interest as she dried a tray of beer glasses. Her eyes darted from Jenny to Nick, the crease of her brow said she didn't like what she saw.

'Nope. This is new for me.' Mrs B. placed Jenny's coffee onto the bar, the ledger catching her eye.

'What's this all about?'

Nick glanced over at Jenny. He knew this was her case, about her family but she was keeping her personal involvement to herself. When Rebecca previously checked up possible dates that Melanie and her Aunt might have visited the Station, Jenny never shared the full story. Maybe now it was time? But what if her boss found out? It was a risk she needed to take.

'You remember when you told me that the people I knew skipped out without paying for their stay – Oh I forgot to offer to pay for that by the way!'

'No need luv. You're paying your dues in law enforcement.' Mrs B. patted her hand, but her eyes lingered on the ledger page. Jenny studied her closely.

'Well, they were my cousin Mel and Aunt Carolyn and they never made it home Mrs B. I've been searching for them ever since.' Mrs B.'s eyes finally found Jenny's. The look of guilt was unmistakable. Jenny's experience interviewing criminals made picking the signs easy. But why would Mrs B. feel guilty?

'Oh luv. Sometimes we should just let these things go. So we can move on.'

It wasn't the first time someone said something similar but Jenny didn't expect it from Mrs B.. The lady was tough as nails – like Marj.

'Would you?' Nick said the words Jenny was thinking. Jenny patted his hand. His tone was annoyed. Just like the day he picked Sam up from the hospital and it was obvious he didn't want to speak with her. The day she realised he didn't think much of the police. Now she understood why.

'It's okay. It's nothing I've not heard before Mrs B. but my family has a right to know if Melanie is alive or dead and if she's dead, I'm going to make sure the person responsible spends the rest of their life behind bars.'

Mrs B.'s eyes drifted back to the ledger.

'Hey, what are you two doing here?' Jenny turned around to see Nev strolling around the corner from the dining room. 'I thought I heard your voice in here.'

'Just grabbing a coffee Nev.'

'Your mate Gavin was in here last night.'

Jenny jumped from her stool... the ledger, her coffee, all forgotten. 'Why didn't you call me?'

Nev looked from Jenny to Nick, then Rebecca. Jenny could see he wasn't sure how much he should say. 'I didn't want to disturb your weekend.'

'This I needed disturbing for. Where is he now?'

Nev shrugged. 'I don't know. Left late last night in a mess, wouldn't you say Mrs B.? All mopey and teary.'

'He wasn't his usual self.' Mrs B. admitted.

'I don't care about his frame of mind. Does anyone know where he went?' Jenny tried unsuccessfully to keep her tone calm.

'Home I'd assume.' Rebecca's hands were on her hips.

'Gavin Murphy has been MIA since last Friday. Oh my god Nev. I wish you'd phoned me.' Jenny's tone was calmer now. She came so close to finding Gavin and now he had slipped through her fingers again.

'Sorry.' Nev stared at his feet. 'Oh. I almost forgot. He got into a fight with an older couple.'

'He did. You're right. The couple whose daughter went missing all that time ago.' Mrs B. wiggled her finger as she spoke.

'Really people!' Jenny rolled her eyes. 'Did Gavin leave with them? After them?'

'Why?' Rebecca's tone told Jenny she was dead right. The woman didn't like her. Or at least didn't like her hanging around with Nick.

'Because Gavin is required for questioning in an ongoing police investigation that I'm not able to discuss with you right now.' Nick and Nev scoffed. Mrs B.'s eyebrow rose. Rebecca huffed. 'So! If you have anything *helpful* to add, please do.'

'I didn't hear the argument. It was more the body language that gave it away.' Nev tried to explain. 'Their voices weren't raised, but the woman pushed Gavin. He left first.'

'Last night, what time?'

'I don't know. When did you call last rounds Mrs B.?'

'Just before midnight.'

'Then he left about eleven forty-five.'

'And the older couple?'

'Straight after him.'

'Shit!' Images of Gavin's head blasted to pieces by Marj's rifle flashed before Jenny's eyes. She knew the Motel owner kept a gun it the vehicle. She borrowed the old Nissan dual cab a couple of times. It should have been under lock and key. She knew now that she should have insisted Marj lock it up. But she hadn't.

Mr and Mrs Thompson wanted revenge for their daughter's death and Gavin, together with a loaded gun stumbled right into their path.

'Do we need to go to the Murphy's?' Nick was on his feet, his coffee forgotten.

'We do, if you can take me?'

'For sure.' Nick reached for the ledger and his keys.

'I just need to call this in to Phillips before we leave and I lose reception.'

Chapter 34

The phone almost rang out before Philips answered. 'Coober Pedy Police. Constable Philips speaking.'

'Hey Philips.' Jenny used his last name, immediately indicating to Danny this was a business call. 'I'm heading to Murphy's place now. Nev stayed at the William Creek Pub last night and saw Gavin arguing with Mrs and Mr Thompson. They've got Marj's Nissan and her rifle is in the back cab.'

'Shit! I've got something you need to know before you head out there.' A few papers rustled and Jenny waited, Mrs B.'s office phone pressed to her ear, Nick standing alert by the door ready to go, her foot tapping uncontrollably.'

'Boss stayed over last night. O'Connell is back in town. I can't get a hold of Sarge. Do you want me to call Murphy's?' Phillips spoke as papers continued to rustle.

Jenny was just about to answer, but Phillips cut her off. 'Here it is. Doc says that Beth's broken bones are definitely not accidental. Don't ask me how they know this stuff, but that's what the report says.'

'Okay. That puts a new slant on things.'

'And Williams. I got a call this morning from a reporter who claims she's investigating this case. I don't usually put any weight in what reporters say but she said that she's spoken with the arresting officer on that DUI in the US.'

'The one where Mr Thompson was let off but lost his job?'

'The very same one. She said that the officer in charge was sure that *Mrs* Thompson was driving. He saw movement in the front seat as he approached the vehicle and the tapes on his patrol unit aren't clear enough to substantiate, but it appeared to him like Mr Thompson took the wheel before he got to the car.'

'Why would he do that?'

'I don't know, but we've not been able to get in contact with the arresting officer to confirm. I've contacted someone I know who might be able to get the details. If I find anything important, I'll call the Boss at the Murphy's.'

'Okay, but don't mention anything to Mr Murphy about Gavin being in the pub last night. He might not have gone home. He could be anywhere.'

Jenny was just about to hang up. 'Williams!'

'Yeah?'

'Just be careful. You haven't got a weapon.'

Jenny watched Nick, wondering if taking him into such a dangerous situation was wise. 'I know. I'll be careful.'

Jenny hung up, her mind racing with questions. Why would *Mr* Thompson take a DUI conviction unless his wife was on her third strike?

'Let's go!' Jenny flew past Nick, down the hall past the kitchen and out into the main dining area.

She could sense Nick right behind her as she jogged outside to Nick's four-wheel drive.

'Do you want to go back and get the chopper?' Nick asked as he slipped into the driver's seat and started the motor.

'How far are we from Murphy's by-road?' Nick pulled out of the driveway, heading toward the intersection that would lead to Nick's home or the road back to Coober Pedy where Murphy's station entrance was.

'It's about the same amount of time either way, but the chopper will give you a vantage point flying in. You'll be able to see which vehicles are on site. Especially if Gavin's car isn't there. We can fly out to the shed or somewhere else and look for him.

Did Nick know what she was thinking? He could probably sense her anxiety.

182

'It could get dangerous Nick. I'm not sure I should be taking you into this situation at all. Marj has a gun in that car of hers and Mr and Mrs Thompson may be on a vigilante hunt for Gavin. Or worse, they could be the reason Beth Thompson ran away to begin with and if that is the case, they could simply want to eliminate Gavin before he tells someone why the girl ran. I've got a horrible feeling it's the second option.'

'I could tell by your body language things were getting serious. I'll grab my rifle when we get the chopper. I'll stay out of the way, but I can cover you in case you need it.'

'Nick. You can't discharge a weapon at another person without facing serious charges, even if you are defending me. You'll be charged.'

'That's a risk I'll take.' Jenny was speechless. It was what she would do for him if the shoe was on the other foot, but she was a trained police officer.

Nick spoke without taking his eyes off the road as they sped toward the Homestead. 'Things work differently out in the bush. Murphy isn't my favourite person in the world, but we are neighbours and out here, having neighbours come to your aid can be life or death.'

He was silent a moment. 'Besides, you've got no back up and I'm not about to stand by and see you harmed. Not even in the line of duty.'

Chapter 35

The chopper circled Murphy's Homestead. The burgundy
Nissan was parked alongside a gun-metal grey Landcruiser
with a foldout canopy built for bush camping.

'That's got to be Gavin's vehicle.' Jenny didn't need to
see the registration number to be sure. It made sense that Gavin
owned a self-contained vehicle. The shed they found, where
Beth was likely living was simple, with no kitchen or toilet
facilities. This set up was geared up for bush camping,
including a roof top tent and probably a pull-out kitchen.

'I can't see Sarge's car, but Philips said O'Connell
returned to Coober Pedy, likely with the police Cruiser.'

'What do you want to do?' Nick's brows furrowed.
Jenny never recalled seeing him so worried.

'We can't land here. We are sitting ducks and I don't
want them to know we are coming.' Her pulse was rising with
adrenalin.

'We just flew low over the property. We might have
already tipped them off.' Nick pulled on the stick and sent the
chopper veering hard right, away from the Homestead.

'I hope not. Fly out of sight, land and I'll go in on foot.'

'That doesn't sound like a good idea.'

The land sped by as the chopper flew low over the
ground. New grass shot up through the barren earth. A sudden
surge from the recent rains gave the land a greenish tinge. She
took a measured breath, forcing her body to relax.

'We have your hand-held UHF radios. I'll call you in if
I need back up. See if you have the range to call in an update to
Philips.'

'I'll call in a mayday. Other radio users in the area can
relay my message.'

'Don't call the cavalry just yet. If you can just get Philips on standby.' Nick nodded, but his solemn expression said he didn't like being left behind.

'You need to take the rifle?'

'I can't. I don't want to raise anyone's hackles. I'm not sure what I'm walking into, but not being in uniform could be an advantage.'

'But don't the Thompsons know you're a cop?'

'Yes, but we could be blowing this all out of proportion. I'll snoop around. Update you on the radio. Don't call in any emergency unless you can't contact me or I ask you to. They could be all sitting down having Devonshire tea for all we know.'

Nick landed the chopper beyond a stand of mallee bushes but kept the rotors spinning and the engine powered up ready to take off.

'Just keep me in the loop. If I get radio silence, I'm calling a state of emergency.'

'You got it.' Jenny ducked as she hopped from the chopper and scurried away to a safe distance before standing upright. She didn't look back. Her stomach was already doing summersaults from the tension. Seeing how worried Nick was wouldn't help.

A few minutes' flight turned out to be a decent distance to jog. Sweat was running down the inside of Jenny's T-shirt by the time she neared the rocky driveway that led to the raised veranda on the front of the Murphy's Homestead.

'Nick. Do you read me? I'm here.'

'Roger. Go ahead.'

The idea that Mr Murphy might have his UHF on in the kitchen suddenly made Jenny reconsider using the radio. How could she let Nick know what was happening without informing Gavin or the Thompsons she was right outside the door?

'I'll get back to you soon. Just give me a minute or two.'

'You have two max.' Jenny was glad Nick kept his communication short.

A tiny piece of green lawn was lost amongst red dirt and sandstone bricks. The sound of voices coming from the house steered Jenny around the Homestead's long covered veranda toward the back of the building.

She crept carefully, her back against the building, her eyes darting from side to side trying to take in every angle all at once.

A creaking floorboard just ahead made her stop, her foot hovered in the air not sure where or if to come down.

A muffled sound made her jump. Was that a sniffle? Jenny listened, the sound of her own breathing and pounding heart was all she could hear for a full ten seconds. Then she heard it again.

She crept forward slowly, wishing in that moment for her gun or Taser. As she ducked under the fold-out clothesline against the wall, she heard the same sound again. To her left was a glass door, sitting ajar. Beyond Jenny could make out slate tiles and just the edge of a washing machine.

Someone was in the laundry room. How on earth was she going to get past without being seen? The sniffing turned into a sob. In that moment, Jenny realised whoever was in the laundry beyond was not going to be a threat to her.

She gently pushed the glass door open. On the floor, her arms wrapped tightly around her legs, her face hidden behind her knees was Anna. The woman was trembling, unwilling to look up for fear that whoever entered, might harm her.

'Anna.' Jenny spoke softly, not sure exactly where the laundry might be in relation to the main living area of the house or where the voices were coming from.

'Don't say anything. It's okay. I'm here. Help is coming.' Anna stared up, suspicion in her gaze.

'Is everyone inside okay?' Anna nodded. 'Is anyone armed?' Another nod. *Shit!* Jenny suddenly wondered over her wisdom to not accept Nick's rifle. *Nick!* She needed to call in. Her two minutes were up, but she was inside the homestead, too close to the conflict to let him answer her over a loud crackling radio.

She turned the volume down and spoke softly. 'I'm okay. Give me another five.' There was no way she knew he heard her, any more than she could hear him, but it was a risk she might have to take.

Should she tell him to call in help? She couldn't risk escalating the situation. Any official help would be miles away. Coober Pedy didn't have a Police helicopter and the closest tactical police support would be Adelaide, Alice or maybe Broken Hill. *Too far.*

'Anna,' she whispered. The woman made fleeting eye contact. Her eyes darted around wildly. How long had she been hiding here? 'Who has the gun Anna? Gavin or Mr Thompson?'

Anna sucked in a deep breath, her whole body shuddered. The trembling finally stopped. 'Mrs!'

'*Mrs* Thompson has the gun?' Jenny kept her voice down to a whisper, but it jumped an octave. She didn't see that coming. 'Have they been here all night?'

'Gavin came home at eight this morning. They arrived about twenty minutes later.'

'Is Sergeant Mackenzie still here?' Anna nodded. 'And no one is hurt?'

'No.'

She patted Anna's knee. 'Stay here. This will be sorted soon. Okay?' Anna nodded, wrapped her arms around her knees again and balled up as small as she could into the corner between the washing machine and the upright freezer.

Jenny's mind was racing as she tried to piece everything together. She knew she needed to move. To get into a position to disarm Suzanna Thompson, but her head was spinning as she asked herself why Mrs Thompson would be tracking Gavin down, armed with Marj's rifle, obviously ready to do some harm.

Philips told her that a reporter claimed the arresting officer in Orange County claimed that Trent Thompson might not have been driving when he was booked for DUI. Then there were all the broken bones Beth sustained when she was young. Her dad was a doctor. He could have set them without anyone knowing. So why didn't he?

Did Beth run away? It was beginning to look that way. It was the only thing that made sense.

'No! Suzanna. No!'

Jenny was moving before she realised it. Bursting through the kitchen door, she tried to get her bearings quickly as adrenalin surged.

Sergeant Mackenzie was unconscious on the floor. Kent Murphy was on his knees next to his friend while Suzanna Thompson waved Marj's rifle, the barrel pointed at Gavin Murphy who was trapped, hard up against the dining table, his hands in the air before his face protectively.

'I never said a word. I swear.'

'You killed my baby!' Suzanna screamed.

'Hold up everyone. Let's take a breather.' Jenny spoke as calmly as she could, moving forward, her hands in the air, her eyes on her unconscious boss, scanning his body for any blood. No shot was fired. Maybe he went down before she got there?

'You stay out of this.' Suzanna was hysterical. The gun waved from side to side with no real purpose or control.

'Suzanna please. This is my fault.' Jenny watched Mr Thompson plead with his wife.

'It's your fault she ran away!' Gavin was screaming now, tears streaming down his face. At first, she thought he was yelling at Mr Thompson. Her brain began to put the pieces together.

'You've been covering for Suzanna for too long Trent.' *Marj is going to be so disappointed she backed the wrong camp.*

'It's not like that.' He pleaded with his eyes.

'Suzanna. Why don't you put down the gun and we can talk through what happened after Beth went missing?'

'I want him dead. He killed my baby.'

'*You* killed your baby!' Gavin sobbed. *He must have cared a lot for Beth. Damn!*

'Did you know she was pregnant?' Jenny needed to distract Suzanna. To get that rifle pointed away from Gavin before she accidentally pulled the trigger.

'What!' The woman spun in her direction.

Jenny saw her boss stir on the floor as Kent helped him to a sitting position. A red welt was already on his forehead.

'Maybe I can put the kettle on and we can work out what happened?' Jenny knew the chances were slim, but she wanted to bring the tension level down a notch and have Suzanna focus on her, not the Murphys.

Gavin opened his mouth to speak, but Jenny shook her head. He closed his lips. She let out a breath. No matter what happened now, she needed to deescalate the situation. It didn't matter who hit Sarge or why.

Maybe he tried to get the gun? Maybe he tried to place himself between Gavin and Suzanna?

Jenny didn't have time to think about it right now. Right now, she needed to get that rifle out of Suzanna's hands.

'My daughter is dead and you want to put the kettle on!' Suzanna's voice oozed loathing.

'Trent.' The former doctor was stunned like a deer in headlights. 'Put the kettle on.' It was a distracting technique and it was working. Suzanna frowned as her husband did as he was asked.

'You've always been weak.' The pageant mum's tone sent a chill down Jenny's spine. It seemed so out of place against the woman's fine clothing, perfect make-up and carefully styled hair.

Even after an evening hunting down Gavin, following him from the pub to wherever he disappeared overnight, to now – the woman presented immaculately. Yet the scathing tone belonged to a demon from some apocalyptic movie.

Jenny stepped between Gavin and Suzanna slowly, further blocking her boss and Kent from the ever-present threat of Marj's rifle.

'Where's your tea kept Kent.' Jenny was amazed her voice didn't waver.

'In the cupboard above the kettle.' Jenny nodded toward the cupboard, encouraging Trent to ignore Suzanna's comment and get on with the job she had given him.

'Can we put the gun down and talk, woman to woman?' Suzanna watched her husband retreat to the kitchen. 'Don't you want to know what Beth has been doing all this time?'

Suzanna's expressions hovered between crazed and confused. Jenny needed to get that gun away from her before crazed took over again.

'You obviously loved your daughter. I've seen all the pageant photos.' Jenny kept her tone calm, gentle, sympathetic. But if she was right, she was speaking with an insane monster.

'She was beautiful. But when she said she didn't want to enter the pageants anymore I could tell she just needed encouragement.'

'It's tricky isn't it. Giving her encouragement and boosting her confidence. That's all you were doing, wasn't it?' Jenny's stomach rolled at the lies.

She knew her five minutes were up. God, she hoped Nick didn't do anything stupid. Gavin was agitated, his foot tapped intermittently as he leant against the dining table, his body rigid. Sergeant Mackenzie rose slowly to sit on the closest chair while Suzanna was distracted.

'But she was a naughty little girl and he just *encouraged* her to *disobey* me.' Suzanna threw an accusatory look at her husband.

The woman was talking freely now. This is what Jenny needed. She watched the gun barrel lower. As Suzanna glared at her husband, Jenny took a quick look at Sarge. His eye was swollen shut but the still open one was wide with focus. He nodded for her to go on.

'A bit of a daddy's girl then?' Jenny forced a light chuckle when inside her emotions were screaming for her to lunge at the woman while the rifle was low and no one was in its sights.

The kettle boiled in the background. A creak on the old floorboards sounded from Jenny's right. Her back was to Gavin, Sarge sat on a chair to her left with Kent Murphy standing alongside. Suzanna Thompson was in front of her, Trent beyond in the kitchen. Who was to her right?

Time stood still as Suzanna's eyes fell on something behind Jenny. She tried to consider what. Someone must have entered the dining room. Anna? Maybe Gavin moved positions. Or maybe, god please no, maybe Nick came inside.

The rifle swung from facing down. Jenny saw the expression on Suzanna's face go hard. Crazy was back. There would be no talking her down now.

As the rifle rose, time slowed. Jenny was vaguely aware of someone screaming at her.

'Move!'

She lunged forward, landing on top of Suzanna as the rifle came up. The shot was fired. The sound ringing in her ears. Jenny scrabbled with the woman beneath her. A feral scream sounded. For a moment, Jenny wasn't sure if it was hers or Suzanna's.

A few seconds dragged as time appeared to cease. Jenny reached for the rifle, ripped it free and threw it behind her to the left. Sergeant Mackenzie snapped it up as Jenny rolled Suzanna over, grabbed her right arm and pinned it behind her back, her knee hard in the woman's back.

Ignoring the woman's protests, Jenny dragged the pageant mum to her feet. She turned, to discover who had startled Mrs Thompson. Nick stared at her from the doorway, his eyes wide with surprise. Jenny flashed him a smile, then watched him crumple to the ground, blood streaming from his chest.

'No!'

Chapter 36

Sergeant Mackenzie tossed the rifle to Kent 'Take this!' He was beside Jenny, taking control of her prisoner in a heartbeat. 'I've got her. You look after him!'

'Nick.' Jenny's heart leapt into her throat as she skidded to her knees beside him. Lifting his shirt, she gasped at the blood oozing too quickly from a wound in his upper right shoulder.

Jenny focussed on Nick as his eyes rolled back in their sockets. Her heartbeat sounded in her ears as her blood drain to her toes. The vague awareness that Mrs Thompson was mouthing off while her husband begged her to be quiet until they got a lawyer fuelled her rage and kept her from crying.

Stay focussed!

'Call in the Flying Doctors.' She yelled over her shoulder to anyone who would listen before ripping off her shirt, scrunching it into a ball and pressing it against the wound.

'Anna!' Murphy yelled. 'Gavin, get on the blower and get the doc here.'

Gavin disappeared without a word.

'Anna. Get the hell in here! Bring the first aid kit.' *How did Kent know she was hiding in the laundry? Maybe he sent her there? Nick needed more than a bandage!*

A thought struggled to the surface over the adrenalin fuelled fear. 'Nev. Nev was at the pub in William Creek this morning.' She saw Mackenzie nod before he tied Mrs Thompson's hands behind her back with a dish cloth. The wince on the fugitive's face did nothing to settle Jenny's nerves.

'Nick! Can you hear me!' No response. 'Nick!' Jenny continued to apply pressure as she held his hand. 'Squeeze my fingers if you can hear me.'

A light tension made her almost squeal. Anna ran into the kitchen, joining Jenny on her hands and knees.

'I need bandages.' They appeared before Jenny finished her sentence.

'Do you want me to inspect?' Jenny resisted the urge to slap Anna's hand away. 'I studied nursing. Only a little while, but I remember some.'

'There's nothing we can do out here.' Jenny studied the wound, which was high on Nick's left shoulder. It was unlikely to have hit a major organ, but the blood. There was so much blood. It could have gone right through a major artery for all she knew.

'We need to keep the pressure on until we get him to a hospital.' Jenny continued applying pressure. 'Don't go far because I need someone who knows CPR if we need it.' *Please don't need it!*

'Yes. Do you need another new shirt?'

Jenny glanced down at her sports bra, thankful it wasn't her black lace number.

'It can wait.'

'Nev is on his way.' Mackenzie returned to the dining room. 'Can I help?' He sounded nervous.

'Not yet.' She knew that applying this much pressure for a long time would fatigue her. If Nick went into cardiac arrest, she wanted to be the one to look after him, but letting go now meant she wasn't in control. *She needed to be in control!*

'Jenny.' The words were softly spoken.

She stared up, surprised Sarge used her first name. 'I can apply pressure. Grab a shirt.'

She hesitated.

'He'll be okay.'

'Plane's in the air.' Gavin skidded to a halt in the dining area. His presence created a fresh tirade from Mrs Thompson and this time, Jenny couldn't hold herself together.

'You!' She stomped toward the woman with purpose. Mr Thompson stepped between them, no doubt sensing what was running through Jenny's mind.

'Constable Williams.' Sarge kept his tone mild, but there was authority in his words.

Jenny stopped, her shoulders sagged, then rose as she slowly and purposefully took a long, steadying breath.

'Mrs Thompson. Sit down, shut up or I'll gag you.'

'You can't...'

Jenny stepped closer. The woman flinched. '*You* are responsible for all of this. Not Gavin, not me and definitely not Nick.'

'I...I.'

'*You* abused your daughter.'

'I never.'

'Multiple fractures, managed at home by your husband so that the alarm bells wouldn't ring. Or maybe he didn't know.' She studied him, her mind still not made up. 'Those poorly managed fractures, that likely needed surgery or at the very least, a plaster cast are the reason why we knew Beth suffered abuse well before she disappeared on your trip here.'

'Please don't do this.' Trent pleaded quietly, his eyes bewildered and filling with tears.

'You did nothing.' She pointed her finger at Beth's father. 'You have covered up for this woman long enough. You said it yourself. Beth wasn't abducted, she ran away and Gavin did his best to care for her.'

'I didn't think anyone would believe us.' Gavin spoke quietly from the doorway, keeping his distance even though Mrs Thompson was clearly restrained.

Jenny stepped over to Gavin, put her hand on his shoulder, patting gently. 'You really should have told someone mate.'

'I know that now, but we thought the police would just send Beth home and then.' His head dropped, the rest of his words left hanging in the thick, uncomfortable atmosphere.

'Come on Gav. We'll head out to meet the plane.' Kent put his arm protectively around his son's shoulder.

'Should we stretcher him out?' Murphy's son looked lost. Why wouldn't he be? He kept Beth Thompson a secret since she was eleven and now she was dead, along with her baby – Gavin's baby.

'We should wait for Nev.' Jenny interrupted their conversation.

The sound of the front door being flung opened reached them. 'Jenny!'

Nev's voice was music to her ears. 'Up the back, in the kitchen.' She sounded shrill and panicked, even to her own ears.

'I've got my gear. Are the RFDS on their way?' Nev appeared rushed, but somehow calm and purposeful. The sight of him took the edge off Jenny's panic.

'Plane is coming in any minute.' Murphy pushed Gavin from the dining room. 'We'll bring them in or do you want him taken to the plane?'

Nev took one look at Nick and shook his head. Jenny's stomach hit the floor. 'He's lost a lot of blood. Moving him isn't a good idea. Tell the doc on board to string up a pack of O negative, ready for arrival.'

'You got it mate.' Murphy slapped Nev on the shoulder and Jenny suddenly thought that she could have misread the man on her first visit.

As though he knew what she was thinking, he winked in her direction. 'He's a tough nut that one. Just like his mother. He'll pull through.'

The reference to Nick's mum seemed genuine, not at all disrespectful to the woman who disappeared without a trace all those years ago. The look Murphy gave her made her think he knew more about Nick's family than he was letting on, but now wasn't the time to ask questions.

Right now, all Jenny needed to do was make sure Nick made it.

'Shit!' Jenny followed Nev's eyes. The doctor rushed to Nick's side as he began to convulse.

'CPR. Does anyone know CPR? I might need assistance.'

'First year nurse. Dropped out.' Anna offered. Nev nodded.

Sarge put his bloodied hand on Jenny's arm. She wanted to be the one to save him, to do the CPR. Sarge was right though. These two people were more qualified than her, but she didn't have to like it.

She pulled her arm free of her Sergeant's hold, frustration evident in her eyes.

'You don't want this to be your last memory.'

A scathing comment was on her lips, but for once she understood her boss was genuinely not having a go at her. He was looking out for her.

But she needed to be doing something, anything or she knew her emotions would take control.

The situation was taken out of her hands as two RFDS team members joined the fight to save Nick's life.

Chapter 37

Jenny sat at her desk, her mind wandering from her computer screen to Nick, and all that blood.

'I need your statement while it's fresh Williams.' O'Connell's voice was gentle, but firm.

Sergeant Mackenzie was in his office writing up his own version of the morning's events. Nev was yet to phone her. That wasn't good news. Her stomach clenched as she recalled loading Nick into the RFDS plane, his limp body on the gurney. The IV pumping blood into his body.

The plane transported him to Adelaide. It was the right place for him to get the surgery and care he needed but it was way too far away.

'How did Nick end up mixed up in all of this?'

'He was supposed to stay in the chopper and only come if I called.' She glanced over at O'Connell, his eyes soft and supportive. 'I didn't call. But he came anyway,' she whispered.

'It is what guys do. They like to play hero.'

'Well it was bloody stupid. It could have gotten him killed.' *It might still!*

'Nev said it was the blood loss, not the position of the injury that was the issue. He's been topped up with blood. He'll pull through. Nick Johnston has dealt with a lot in his short life. This won't keep him down.'

Jenny fought back tears. 'Thanks.'

'Hurry up and finish that report. I want you to conduct the final interviews. What tipped you off about Suzanna Thompson anyway?'

'At first I thought they were out for blood, you know some sort of vigilante crusade. Hunt down the guy responsible for their daughter's abduction, but when Philips found out that the arresting officer thought that Trent may have covered for his wife on the DUI, I started to put pieces together. Like the autopsy report which stated multiple fractures from *before* the abduction, all badly healed. That seemed strange when her dad was a doctor.'

'Keep typing, we'll interview the Thompsons separately, then we need to talk to Gavin.'

'Poor kid. I feel sorry for him.'

'Tough call too. He might face manslaughter charges over this.'

'Really! He was only a kid himself when he took Beth in.'

'Let's get your statement, then we can find out what went through his head.

****

Jenny sat opposite Gavin. Two hours of interviews with the Thompsons confirmed everything they already knew. Trent admitted to covering up his wife's mental illness for years. When Beth went missing, he was sure she just ran away.

But there was something niggling at the back of Jenny's mind. So far, she couldn't put her finger on it.

'Gavin, state your full name for the record.' She pointed to the recording equipment. Kent Murphy sat by his son's side. To her surprise, a lawyer wasn't present.

Gavin's hands fidgeted in his lap as he spoke for the recording.

'How old were you when you first met Beth Thompson?'

'Fifteen.'

'Where did you meet her?'

'At the William Creek Pub.'

'Did you encourage her to run away from there?'

'No! It wasn't my idea. None of this was my idea.' Gavin's voiced trailed off.

'So it was Beth's idea? She was only eleven Gavin.'

Gavin took a deep breath, as though something heavy was laying on his chest.

'I was given money.'

'Money!' O'Connell joined the questioning, a look of astonishment crossed his face but he hid it quickly.

'Yeah.'

'So you weren't attracted to Beth?' Jenny pushed.

'She was eleven. To me she was just a kid.'

'Who paid you to take her Gavin?'

'It was anonymous.'

Jenny shook her head as Kent Murphy spoke. 'I think we need that lawyer now.'

'I think that might be a good idea.' O'Connell agreed.

A thought popped into Jenny's head, causing her to push for more. 'Just one more question.' She didn't wait for a reply. 'You were only fifteen Gavin. I can understand a bit of cash would have been handy, but you kept Beth for six years. Were you still getting money?'

'Enough.' Kent Murphy interrupted, but he was too slow.

'Yes!' Gavin answered, his dad scowled. Gavin shrugged as if to say *What!*

'Okay. You don't have to say another word but I think I have an idea what went on.'

'I said that's enough.' Kent pushed his chair back ready to leave.

'We'll be holding Gavin, unless you let me finish Mr Murphy. If you let me finish we might be able to let him go on bail in your care.'

Kent Murphy slowly sat back down. 'You talk.' He pointed to Jenny. 'You stay quiet.' He shook his finger at his son who nodded vigorously in response.

'My guess is Gavin spoke to Trent Thompson at some stage during their visit. He knew the only way to help his daughter without harming his wife was to get Beth to safety. He must have known Gavin was the son of a big land holder in the area. What he didn't think through was that Gavin wasn't the brightest choice and didn't take Beth to his family, like he should have.'

No one seemed offended by the reference to Gavin's level of intelligence.

'Trent Thompson paid you money to "help" Beth run away. I'm guessing, but I'm sure a search of bank records will confirm, that he topped up your bank balance a few times over the years to ensure his daughter got everything she needed.'

Gavin stared at his dad, begging the man to let him confirm or deny her claims, but instead he asked the question that was next on Jenny's list.

'Why didn't you bring the girl to me?'

'I thought you'd be angry with me.'

'So you kept her in a shed?' There was a long silence as Kent Murphy slowly took calming breaths while Gavin teetered on the verge of tears.

'She told me her story Dad. Why she ran away. She didn't know her dad was paying for her to leave home.'

'Why didn't you tell her?' O'Connell asked.

'He wanted the money.' Jenny answered for him.

'Why didn't Trent give her up for adoption?' O'Connell asked.

'Why not get his wife the help she needed and protect his daughter?' Jenny countered. 'He's a coward, that's why.'

'So what happens now?' Kent Murphy glanced from O'Connell to her and back again.

'Now we throw the book at both Suzanna and Trent Thompson. They'll likely face charges in their own country.

The rules are different over there but conspiracy to commit kidnapping, child endangerment possibly a few other charges will be raised against Trent. Suzanna will likely be put into care. She's definitely got a few screws loose.'

'What happens to me?' Gavin leant forward across the interview table.

'We'll let your dad post bail. You're not a threat to anyone now, but you'll face charges. We'll let the magistrate work out what they'll be, considering your age when all this started.'

O'Connell's summary was dispassionate, which was odd for him. Jenny wanted to soften the blow a little, but there was no doubt Gavin was going to have a police record after this. His actions, or inaction led to Beth's death.

'Gavin, you didn't hold Beth against her will, but she was a minor – one you were paid to keep from the world. You took money to keep her hidden.'

'We talked about it.'

'When?'

'Lots. Not at first. I was a kid, but as she got a bit older I told her I could take her to the farm. I could explain but she was so afraid dad or the police would send her home.' Gavin let the rest remain unsaid.

'If all that is true, and it's going to be hard to substantiate, then the judge will be lenient and you'll likely get a suspended sentence. Your job over the next month or so is to gather as much evidence as you can to corroborate your story. Start with your mates who seemed to know Beth under an alias and spent time with you together.'

Kent Murphy was nodding understanding as Jenny's phone rang. She checked the caller ID, then pushed back from the table to stand.

'You right to finish up here?' She showed O'Connell the screen. He nodded.

'Constable Williams is leaving the interview room.' She heard him speak for the recording as she closed the door and answered her phone.

'Penny!' Her head swam. She gripped the doorframe.

'Take a breath.' Her friend sounded calm. It was a good sign. Or maybe it was a bad one.

'Nick?'

'I've been pacing the waiting room for the past hour. This proxy girlfriend stuff is hard work.'

'Is he okay?' Jenny totally missed the relationship reference in her panic.

'He's out of surgery. Prognosis is good. He'll be home buzzing you around to another crime scene in no time.' Penny's voice sounded jubilant. Jenny's heart skipped a beat.

'I wish I could be there.'

'I bet he wishes you could be too.'

****

Thanks for reading! I hope you enjoyed *Her Broken Bones*. I'd love to see your review on your favourite online bookstore.

Her Scorched Bones - Book 3 in the *Opal Field* series is available from all good bookstores now. If you would like to learn more about my writing or what's next in Jenny's story, then visit my website www.atime2write.com.au or you can follow me on Facebook and Instagram.

Made in United States
North Haven, CT
17 March 2024

50110427R00125